Grandad's Extraordinary Camper Van

by John Parsons

2018

By the author

Young Adult Fiction

Ten Quests (Scott series)
Ten Kingdoms (Scott series)
Ten Elements (Scott series)
Those Among Us
Those Among Us Return
Grandad's Extraordinary Camper Van

Grandad's Extraordinary Camper Van

Written and illustrated

by John Parsons

2018

Grandad's Extraordinary Camper Van

Imprint Digital, UK
Cataloging information
ISBN: 978-1-999684-80-8

Credits
Editor: Nicci Robinson @ Global Wordsmiths
Production Design: Nicci Robinson @ Global Wordsmiths

Acknowledgements

My thanks to Jennifer, my wife, for her help, patience, and guidance on the making of this book.

Special thanks also to my editor, Nicci, who read it and did so many corrections, without whom this book would never have been in my readers' hands.

To my son, Steven, who is always there if I call for help, and Vicki, his lovely wife. Also to my daughter, Tracy, who never fails to amaze me, and Quinton, her clever husband. Then to my four grandchildren, Ethan, Theo, Ailsa, and Darcy, who are dying to read this, their Gramphy's "secret book."

Lastly, but most importantly, you my reader, who paid for this story. If you like it, tell your friends, because I should like to write another adventure, but only you can make this possible.

Dedication

For my ever loving wife, Jennifer, who puts
up with so much and helps lift my spirits
when the dark days come.
Remember, all things are possible!

Author's Note

Moon island is my imagination running riot. Such places do exist, and it's possible to feed the stingrays on some island resorts in the Seychelles. As I've done this, it comes highly recommended as a "must do" on anyone's bucket list.

Lastly Nifty. I had a germ of an idea, and it grew when I saw my son-in-law's parents with their camper van. If you own any make or model of camper van, please don't call it Nifty and expect it to do things as it does in the book.

But then again, anything is possible!

John

CONTENTS

Grandad's Extraordinary Camper Van   1

Preparations   11

The Camper Van is Found   13

The Van Has a Secret   19

New Discoveries   25

A Surprise   29

What Next?   37

Another Testing Time   45

About a Funeral   53

Good-bye, Grandad Rowland   59

A Few Surprises   63

Messing About on the River   73

A Letter From the Past   83

Two Weeks Passing   91

Getting There   97

Ashes to Monks   105

Tiger Lodge   119

Visiting Everest   127

A Family Reunited   135

Returning Home   143

One Toot or Two   149

The Secret Beach   157

Another Day   169

Chapter One
Grandad's Extraordinary Camper Van

It has got to be said that Grandad Rowland was very weird. He was one of those people that we saw once a year at Christmas time when the family were forced to go with our mother to deliver a gift of a tin of biscuits and a card.

Not that Grandad Rowland was our grandad. He was Mum's grandad, but we were told to call him Grandad.

Now you may be wondering who we are!

Let me introduce you to my family.

My name is Daniel Short. Most people call me Danny, and I'm eleven. My sister is called Elizabeth, shortened to Belle by friends and sometimes by Mum and Dad. She's nine.

Elizabeth and I get on really well despite the eighteen months between us. We never compete against each other for attention. This may be because we have wonderful parents. I don't think either one of us feel one was more loved than the other, so Elizabeth and I are more in sync with each other than most kids our age.

Mum's name is Wendy, and my dad's name is George. I know how old they are, but Mum has told us to never tell anyone their age...

Since he lived in a crumbling house on the corner of our road, your next question will most likely be "Why did we only see him once a year?" Grandad Rowland was a grumpy old man who hated people, especially those who visited him. "Don't need them. Don't want them to call," he would say to Mum. But she ignored him and always called down to see him at least once each month. He said to Mum that callers interfered with his holiday plans but to the family's knowledge he never went anywhere. He only allowed all of us to visit on one day a year to deliver our Christmas gift, and *that* was never refused.

My mother had hopes that one year he would say thank you, but each year he would just say, "Bring it in, put it on the table, and I will open it on Christmas Day."

We would go into the house and make our way to the front room. The curtains were always drawn, making everything dark, but once our eyes adjusted to the dim light, we could see lots of strange things standing in and around the room.

We were told to sit down on the old sofa and not touch anything. We looked around at strange carvings in all sorts of colours, free-standing around the room.

One looked like an American Indian totem pole, another was a stone face stood behind the sofa with its menacing face looking down on us. Stuffed birds and animal heads hung from the walls, each gathering dust and cobwebs. A boomerang lay on the floor by his chair.

Mum would tell him about our year, the ups and downs, and how we were doing at school, but he just sat in his chair and said nothing. We didn't move. He scared us as he sat there holding his walking stick under his chin that rested on his hands. He just sat holding the cane and staring at us both. I don't think we even breathed in case he thought that was offensive.

Behind him was a stack of boxes and a large spear that leaned against the wall gathering dust, year in, year out.

Mum would offer to come in to clean for him and to wash any clothes he needed doing, but he just shook his long hair and said, "Don't bother. I'm fine as I am." The conversation, such as it was because it was only Mum trying to make any, would end.

We would just look at him. He would offer no words and simply continue to stare at us.

After a long silence, Dad would stand and say, "Why don't you come to our house for a Christmas dinner with us?" He said the same thing every year, but the invitation was always refused with the response, "I'm fine on my own," and we would leave.

But this year was different.

We were told that Grandad Rowland had died, and we would not be going to see him ever again. I don't know if Belle and I were happy about the news or just relieved, but both Mum and Dad seemed to be upset that the old man had died. Mum had found him sat in his chair with his walking stick.

When the police and ambulance people came, Grandad Rowland was confirmed dead and had been for some time. Later, he was removed from the house, and the doctors who do tests to check why people had died said he had died of cancer and it had progressed to many parts of his body.

Mum and Dad started talking about a funeral and who, other than Mum, would take care of it?

The next day a letter arrived addressed to my mum. Mum opened it and read it.

"It's a letter from a solicitor. I'm named in

Grandad's will as his next of kin. They want me to make an appointment to see them."

"Your grandad has made a will?" asked Dad.

"What's a will, Dad?" Elizabeth asked.

"It's like a wish. Before someone dies, they write down who'd they like to leave their house or money to. Grandad's done that and put Mum's name on it. That's roughly what a will is all about."

"Why couldn't he just tell Mum what he wanted?" I asked. "Why write it down?"

"Good question, Daniel. Writing it down makes it legal. If it wasn't, then anyone could just say, 'I want that,' and take it."

"Oh, so Mum has a letter to collect from this man who kept it until Grandad Rowland died."

"Not quite, Elizabeth. He's the legal bit, and he's going to read it to your Mum, and to us if we can go with her."

I lifted my hands and said, "But, Dad, doesn't he know Mum can read for herself?"

"I'm sure he's aware of that, Daniel, but he's required to read it out loud and for all who are with Mum to hear."

"Sounds stupid to me."

"Yes, I suppose it does. But it's been done like this for a long time, and it's not going to change in the near future. Now shall I ring them, Wendy, or would you like to?"

"Would you do it, George? And find out if we can all go."

Dad rang the solicitors and asked if he could come with Mum to hear what the content of the will was all about. The solicitor confirmed that would be fine and asked Dad to bring me and Belle as we were also named. Dad was asked to bring proof of identity for all of us. He also said that it was important that all four of us came, although Mrs Wendy Short, nee Rowland, was the main beneficiary.

We went to bed that night puzzling over what Grandad Rowland could want us there for. We were sure it would be mega boring!

We went on with our day to day existence, with the usual chaotic rush in the morning to get our school things up together. Dad forgot something as usual, his mobile phone or his comb. He always remembered where he had put it the night before but insisted someone must have moved it, and that was why he couldn't find it! Of course, he found it once he put his coat on, but he never remembered putting it there! This happened at least one day on most weeks.

Mum walked with us to school knowing that once we were there and Dad was on his way to work, the morning rush was almost over. She would watch us go into the school and with a little wave, she would smile and walk away.

On Saturday morning a week later, we went with our parents to Plumbers solicitors to hear the contents of Grandad Rowland's will.

Worst of all, we had to dress up in our best clothes!

I had put on my jeans, but as soon as I came into the lounge, Mum told me to change them. Mum was having no arguments, and so, with my best shirt on, school tie on, trousers with a crease in them, and hair combed until she was happy with it, I joined the rest of the family in the car and journeyed down town to the solicitor's office.

Dad spoke to a lady at a desk in the reception, as Mum told me off for running my fingers around the shirt collar.

We waited a few minutes, then a buzzer on the

lady's desk rang and she told us that Mr Plumber would see us now.

She escorted us down a corridor, then knocked on a door, opened it and said, "Please go in."

Four chairs had been placed in front of the desk that Mr Plumber rose from behind. He came around to the front and held out his hand to Mum as the lady shut the door. *Was she frightened we might try to escape?* The room looked like a library, books were on shelves from the top to bottom of the huge unit. They looked almost as old as their owner.

Mr Plumber looked as if he was a hundred years old. He had snow-white hair and grey coloured skin that seemed to have more wrinkles on it than smooth. His nose was huge, his eyes small, and he was dressed in a black suit, with a white shirt, and a black bow tie.

He shook Mum's hand, then Dad's, and then turned to us.

"You must be Daniel," he said to me as he extended his hand for me to shake.

I took it and he bounced it up and down a few times then let it go.

"And you must be the lovely Elizabeth," he said to my sister.

She took his hand and as he bounced it around in his version of a hand shake, I noticed Mum looking at me. I stopped running my fingers around my shirt neck, but when she wasn't looking, I loosened my tie, undid the top button of my shirt, and immediately felt like I could breathe again.

Mr Plumber retreated back around his desk and asked us to be seated as he pointed to the chairs in front of him.

Once we were seated, he sat down and pulled himself towards the desk. His seat must have had wheels on because the seat moved in quite easily.

He opened a folder, looked at its contents for a moment, then looked up at us again.

"First, I must tell you that the body of my client, Mr Albert Rowland, is at the funeral directors on the High Street, waiting for you to arrange the date for the funeral. Mr Albert Rowland made all arrangements for the costs prior to his demise, and once the will has been read, you can call upon them, to make the final arrangement."

He passed over a sheet of paper to my mother.

"This is my letter for the release of Mr Albert Rowland into your care." He turned a page over in the folder. "I will now read the will." He cleared his throat. "This is the last will and testament of Albert Rowland: 'I, Albert Rowland, presently of 2 Willis Way, Winstanton, Herefordshire, England, do hereby revoke all former testamentary dispositions made by me and declare this my last will and testament.'"

After listening to those few lines, I switched off. *Boring or what?* Mr Plumber droned on and on while I looked at a spider making a web from the corner of the room down to some books. It climbed up and down, then around and around, and soon had made a sizeable web.

I had been so busy watching the spider, that when Mr Plumber said, "and that is the end of the reading of the will," I stood up expecting everyone else to get up and leave. How wrong was I? Everyone glared at me, so I sank back into my seat. I felt my cheeks burn as if a thousand red ants had nibbled on them.

"If you have a question, young man, you are quite welcome to ask. You don't need to stand to do so," said Mr Plumber.

"Um, err, no," I muttered.

"Well, then," said Mr Plumber. "In essence, you, Mrs Short, and your family inherit everything as long as you comply to the one bequest made by Albert."

"But I don't understand," Mum said. "You haven't mentioned a bequest."

"Ah, yes. The letter."

Mr Plumber passed a letter across to my mother. "I'm aware of the contents of the letter, and I'm charged to check that you abide by the bequest now and always. It is rather unusual but quite in order. Your failure could result in the repayment of all money to the charity named as second beneficiary should you fail to do so, that being the World-Wide Fund for Nature."

My mother looked at Mr Plumber then at the letter. "Do I open it now?" she asked.

"Oh, most certainly. It's the main condition attached to the inheritance."

Mum opened the envelope and pulled out a yellow piece of paper. This was a proper letter, not typed on a computer but written in the *old* way, with pen and ink.

She sat reading the short message, then looked at Mr Plumber. She then read the letter once again.

"Am I reading this correctly? He wants me to keep his camper van and move it from his garage, putting it in my garage, and to never clean it, paint it, or service it, or change it in any way, nor use it to store things. Why? And what camper van? Has he got one somewhere in his garage? Oh, this is so stupid. Is this a joke made by him? This surely can't be a legal requirement."

We were all looking at Mum as she said this. Belle mouthed "camper van" to me, and I just shrugged.

This was very weird.

Mr Plumber cleared his throat with a sound like humph. "I assure you, Mrs Short, this is quite legal. All you need to do is move his camper van into your garage and just leave it there. Do nothing to it and you keep everything else and do with it what you want. This was his special gift to you and the family."

"But why? If he's got this vehicle in his garage, why must we keep that, and only that, locked in our garage for the rest of our lives?"

"Because you've been nominated as guardian of the said vehicle. He must have thought a lot of it."

"But, Mr Plumber, it also says, 'Use this for holidays.' If we can't maintain the vehicle, and it's bound to need something at some point, how do we go about doing that? This really is nonsense."

"The camper van was the special piece of the bequest. The practicalities of it are of no concern to me. I see many strange requests but don't get involved in the execution of the bequests. I just need to make sure that all aspects of the will are carried out."

Mum looked again at the letter. "If we did this but then moved, we could leave it in the garage for the new people to have."

"No, it doesn't work like that. You're the guardian, and it must move with you."

Mum looked at Dad.

He shrugged. "Well, we do have a double garage

and only one car. I could move the lawn mower and some of the other bits to make room for it."

"Well, if that's settled, all that remains is for you to sign these forms and everything is yours. I have dealt with the probate side of things and will provide you with the necessary documentation to sign to allow me to clear this, acting on your behalf. The estate is not estimated to be over the inheritance limits, so it is only the costs incurred as arranged by my client. He lodged twenty thousand pounds to cover all costs, so a refund will be made once we conclude all the paperwork. I will give you a call after the funeral, for me to come and see that the vehicle is in your garage, not being used for storage, as I will one year from that date. After that, my services will be over."

Mum, who seemed slightly dazed, signed the papers, and we all said goodbye to Mr Plumber.

What a strange morning, but what was to happen now?

Chapter Two
Preparations!

We returned home very quiet, each with questions going on in our minds. Mine was on the spear that leaned against the wall behind the seat Grandad Rowland used to sit in. I wondered if Dad would let me have it.

We arrived home and went into our house.

Dad said, "Well, if we have got to accommodate this van, I had better start sorting the garage out now. Daniel, come and give me a hand."

"Do I have to, Dad? I'd rather play on my Xbox."

"I'm sure you would, but you are now part of my team, clearing up the garage, and there is no get out clause!'

It was no good arguing. If Dad made his mind up on something and I was involved, then it was better to just do it and get in his good books.

I pulled the BBQ and lawnmower out onto the drive and picked up the brushes and tree cutters. A box with a few bathroom tiles was then put out, followed by a bag of netting to go over the blackcurrants to stop the birds eating them. Next, I found two cardboard boxes filled with flower pots.

Dad and I removed the ladder then some long

canes.

The garage was looking quite clear now.

Dad went over to the work bench in the other garage and found some wall hooks to fix on the wall. He drilled the holes. I found the small folding steps and pushed the wall plugs in and hit them in with the hammer. Dad fixed the hooks onto the wall.

We hung the ladder on two of the hooks, then lifted the lawnmower and hung it by its handles. We put a tall wooden box in one corner and put the tree cutters and a few other tall things in it. Slowly we hung or contained things back into corners of the garage.

I swept the garage out, collected the dust, and put it in the rubbish bin.

Dad had made some shelves, so we stacked the flower pots on them for Mum to have easy access.

"Now we're all ready for Grandad's camper van," I said, surveying our afternoon's work proudly.

Chapter Three
The Camper Van Is Found

I woke on Sunday morning knowing that we would be going down to Grandad's house to find the camper van.

Breakfast was eaten very quickly, and Mum said we could leave the dishes until we returned as she wanted, like us, to find out about the camper van.

We all walked down the road to Grandad's house, and once we arrived, Mum opened the front door with the key she had been given by Mr Plumber.

We walked into the corridor, then into the front room like we always did at Christmas.

Grandad's chair was in the same place. Everything was the same, except Grandad wasn't there. His walking stick was leaning against the chair almost as if it was waiting for him to come back. The boomerang was still by his chair.

"Would you open the curtains, darling?" Mum asked. "Let's have some light on the job."

My eye was on the spear! As the sunlight came through the window, it fell on the spear point and a rainbow reflected from it. The point of the spear was almost on fire with the light.

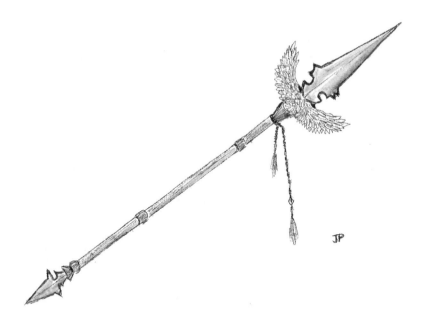

We all looked around the room and saw the colours of the stuffed birds had come alive. Pity the birds still had no life in them. The light shone on a stack of framed butterflies with magnificent tones all glowing on their wings.

Dad said, "This room looks better with natural light on it. Let's go into the back room and see what's waiting for us there."

We followed Dad out of the room and into the back. Pots of plants, with huge leaves and a mass of flowers were crammed into this room with only a narrow pathway between the plants to allow any access. Grandad had laid a thick polythene sheet onto the bare floorboards then put small stones on top. The plants stood in big square pots, and roots were coming out of the base of some plant pots.

The narrow pathway allowed one person to walk

into the room under the plants. Some were bending over having grown up to the ceiling. This must be how Grandad had watered his plants. It was like walking into a jungle.

He pointed to the large plants that looked like trees. "They're bromeliads. Their roots hanging down to take in moisture, and it was unusual to see them like this."

"Why are they on a plant, Dad? Are the roots going to come down to the floor?"

"No, Daniel, they're called 'Air plants,' and these are very good and healthy looking plants."

Mum, ever practical, said, "How are we going to clear all this out? It can't stay like this if we're going to sell the house."

We left the greenhouse room and went into the kitchen.

"Well, at least this room is normal," said Mum. "But it looks as if Grandad didn't clean up after any of his meals. Look at the stacked piles of takeaway boxes, and he has only one plate and one knife and fork."

She opened drawers that were empty but found some cupboards were full of powdered feed for tropical plants. The fridge was empty, as was the freezer. They weren't even switched on.

We found pots and pans, quite rusty from not being used, and plastic boxes and bowls in another cupboard. But when Mum touched one of the plastic bowls, it crumbled, cracked, and broke.

"Everything in here must go," said Mum, sounding exasperated. "Oh dear, it's going to take forever to tidy this place up."

"Don't fret, Wendy," said Dad. "We're just assessing what's to be done. We'll soon get this sorted, and someone will jump at the chance to live here once we're finished with it."

Mum just looked at him, then sighed, and unlocked and opened the kitchen door to go into the garage.

As we all stepped down two steps into the garage, we were amazed. It was super clean. Not a bit of dust could be seen. All the tools were neatly organised, and the walls and ceiling were all painted cream.

In the middle of the garage stood the light blue, rusty camper van.

"So, this is what all the fuss is about," said Dad as he walked up to it.

"But it's rubbish," said Belle as she walked up to it and reached out to run her hand along it. "Just look at the rust on it."

"Don't touch it, Elizabeth. You don't know what sort of tramps have lived in this. It's such an awful thing." She turned to Dad. "George, do we really need to keep it?"

"I guess the question is, do you want to accept your Grandad's wishes and the money he has left you? If you do, we have to accept this as a gift to the family."

"I wonder what's inside it, can we open the vans doors and look inside?" I asked.

"Is it locked?"

I took hold of the door handle and opened it.

"No," I called out as I looked inside.

The seats looked as if they were new. The dashboard was shiny and showed little sign of use, and a key hung in the ignition, waiting to be turned.

I climbed up into the back part of the camper van. Again, this looked brand new. The cooking unit looked as if it had never been used. The seats were perfect. Everything inside was.

"This is blooming weird," I said. "Outside it's a pile of junk, yet inside it all looks brand new." I turned and called out to the others, "Take a look at this, you're not going to believe it. If this isn't strange, then nothing is."

Dad ducked in and sat on one of the seats, and Mum joined him. Elizabeth climbed into the driver's seat and turned sideways on it to look in on us.

"Well, I must say that this is really quite a surprise. From the outside, it looks a wreck, but inside it's rather nice. A little squashed up, but nice."

"But how can it be so new inside and a load of crud outside?" I asked

"Everything about this is mystifying," said Mum.

"I wonder if your grandad ever did go in this on holidays. Do you think it was just sentimentality that he put in the clause for us to keep it?" asked Dad.

"Well, if he did go on holiday in it," Mum said as she wiped her finger across a clean window, "I don't know how he kept it in good condition inside."

Elizabeth leaned out of the camper van and pulled the door shut. Just as the door banged shut, the camper van started to shake...

Chapter Four
The Van Has a Secret!

"Elizabeth, did you turn the key in the van to start the engine?" Dad called out loudly as he tried to get to the front.

"No, I didn't. I just closed the door."

"Open it quickly and get out. I'm coming to see what's happening."

As Belle opened the door again, the shaking stopped. Dad reached the front seat just as she stepped down to the garage floor.

"Well, just to be safe, let's not leave this here." He pulled the key out.

"Can I get in with Mum and Daniel to see what it's like in the back please?" she asked.

"Yes, it's all fine now. Go around through to the rear and try the seats there. I think you'll like it."

Elizabeth walked around to the other side and opened the door. She climbed in and pulled the door shut.

Dad pulled the driver's door shut and again, as it slammed shut, the van began to shake and tremble, and Elizabeth scrambled into Mum's arms.

As it shook, strange things began to occur; the roof lifted, the sides expanded out, and the van got longer and longer. Soon it was as if we were sat in our lounge. Then it stopped.

I was feeling quite shocked and a little dazed. What had just happened? Was this a magic van?

I looked at everyone else. Elizabeth was holding onto Mum who was sat with her mouth open, and Dad was scratching his head in amazement.

"I have no idea what has just happened but the rest of the garage looks the same. What's it like at the back, Danny?"

I got up to look out of the rear window. I could see the rest of the garage, just as it was, and the two steps from the kitchen into the garage. "It's just the same, Dad," I called out.

Dad got out of the van, leaving the driver's door open and walked down to us. He opened the rear door and got in and sat down on the seat, next to Mum and Elizabeth.

"I feel rather strange," he said. "Could we all be hallucinating? Have some of those plants drugged us?"

"Oh, George, don't say that. There must be another answer."

"I can't think of another answer, other than maybe it's—"

"Magic," I said and waved my hand in the air like I had a wand.

"Nonsense," said Mum. "Next you'll be saying it's a space ship or something."

She got out of the van and we all joined her. We could see the inside of the van, very big and spacious, but from the outside, it just looked like the same scruffy camper van.

"It's like a Tardis," said Dad. "It looks small on the outside but it's bigger on the inside."

"It definitely grew. We all saw that. The blooming

weird thing is it has only grown on the inside, it's just as if it's in two parts."

"I do wish you wouldn't say blooming, Daniel. It's weird but certainly not in any respect blooming!"

Dad went around and looked in the opened driver's door again.

"Elizabeth, will you shut the sliding door, please," asked Dad.

Elizabeth did as Dad asked and stepped back quickly from the van.

"Nothing's happened," shouted Dad. He climbed back down and shut the door.

"This is strange," he said. "I don't know how that just happened, but it did. One thing's for sure, this van is not staying here. I'm getting it moved to our garage as soon as I can so I can investigate."

We went back into the house and tramped upstairs. The three bedrooms were full of souvenirs from all around the world; tribal axes, boxes of shells and rocks, flags, jugs, masks, plates, and even a life belt with Titanic on it.

"What a load of old junk," said Mum. "It can't be authentic, surely." She pointed to the life belt.

"We're going to need some experts to view this stuff. I have no idea if any of it is worth a penny or a pound," Dad said as he looked around.

Folders were stacked in one room. Mum opened one and looked to be scanning it.

"This has a list of places that he has possibly been to around the world," she said and handed the folder to Dad.

"When did he do that?" asked Dad.

"I have no idea, but he's got a list of all the things he has brought back from his visits."

"Look, let's call it a day and go home. I'm hungry;

what about you lot?"

"I'm ready for some food too, Dad. This exploring seems to make me hungry."

Belle laughed and said, "Danny, you're always hungry."

"I don't know about the rest of you," said Mum, "but I need to sit down. This has been quite an experience."

"Grandad's camper van certainly shook us all up," said Dad.

We all laughed at the panic it had caused. We went downstairs, locked the door to the garage in the kitchen, then left through the front door of Grandad's house and walked home.

I took my shoes off before going into the lounge. That was a rule never to be broken on pain of Mum's wrath!

"I think we should just give everything to the charity," said Mum. "It's going to be a lot of work to sort the house out, and I could do without it."

"But the camper van, Mum," I said. "If it is magic, then we should see what else it can do."

"I agree," said Dad. "And if we concentrate on clearing one room at a time, it will soon be cleared."

"But it's so much hassle, and I think we'll have to pay people to take it away. I'd rather just give it to charity," said Mum.

"But if Grandad wanted a charity to have the house and the camper van, he would've given it to them and not you," I said.

"That's true. What I don't understand is all this magic stuff," said Mum. "It's blowing my mind. That van expanded, but when we got out it was just a normal size. It's impossible."

"I bet Grandad knew it was a magic camper

van and that's why he wanted you to have it," said Elizabeth.

"You always said Grandad was a strange man. If you thought he never went anywhere, how did he go to all of those places on his list and collect all of those souvenirs in his house?" I asked.

"Wendy, let's not worry for the moment. We don't even know if it's magic. Maybe it was something to do with all those unusual plants."

I looked at Elizabeth and tried not to laugh.

"Let's talk about dinner," said Dad.

"Shall we have a Chinese takeaway?" asked Mum. "We can all pick one dish and try lots of different dishes."

"That sounds yummy," said Elizabeth.

"Absolutely," I said. "Sounds great."

"Okay. I'll get the menu. Remember, Daniel, don't pick any hot and spicy dishes. You know how they affect your father!"

I couldn't get Grandad's house of mystery out of my mind. What other things would we discover?

Chapter Five
New Discoveries

The next day, we went to school, but both Elizabeth and I admitted we found it hard to concentrate on our lessons and that we went through Grandad's house in our minds!

Mum met us at the school gates, as she always did. I was dying to ask the question that Belle and I had talked about.

"Are we going to go down to Grandad's house again to start sorting out his stuff?" I asked.

"Well, not just yet," said Mum. "I've been down to the funeral directors and made the arrangements for a date for the funeral. And I went to the bank to close Grandad's bank account with the letter from Mr Plumber. They showed me the amount he has left us. We won't be millionaires, but we will be able to go on some holidays abroad."

"So will that mean that we'll be getting an increase in our pocket money as our share, Mum?" I asked.

"Now that sounds like a plan, big brother."

Mum raised her eyebrows. "I'm sure it does. However we can talk about that later. Now, where was I?"

"You'd just found out how much was in the

bank," I said, "and how we could go abroad for some holidays."

"Ah, yes." Mum nodded. "Next I went to the estate agents to get a rough idea of the cost of three-bedroomed houses in our area."

"So, we're keeping the camper van?" I asked, desperate for Mum to say yes.

"And the money," added Belle.

"It looks like it. Both you and your father seem very keen to do that, so once all the legal bits are done, we'll sort it out."

Elizabeth and I grinned at each other. *Excellent news.*

"Your dad rang me this morning from work and said he wants to go to the house again this evening to try to start the camper van. If he can, he'll drive it to the house."

"Can we go with him, Mum?" Belle and I asked at almost the exact same time.

"You have homework to do, don't you? I think it's best that your dad drives it home by himself...just in case."

"But, Mum, he might want some help," I said. "I could open and shut the garage doors."

"He might want my help, too," said Elizabeth. "If he drops the van key under the van, I'm small enough to get under it."

I looked at Belle and grinned. She was once again in sync with me, we both wanted to see the van again. If something else happened, we wanted to be there.

"You need not think you're fooling me, but I suppose it won't hurt to join Dad when he starts the van. But you're not going inside it, in case something goes wrong!"

We arrived home, and Mum unlocked the door.

"Okay, off you go with your homework, and if you get it all finished in time, we'll all go down to Grandad's house and help your dad sort out the camper van."

I punched the air and grinned. "Understood, Mum," I said. I patted Belle on the shoulder. "Let's go!" We rushed up the stairs to get started on our homework.

It was almost two hours later when Dad came home. Elizabeth and I shot downstairs.

"We're coming with you, Dad," I said. "We've both done most of our homework, and Mum said we could all go down to Grandad's house to see you start the van."

"Did she now? Well, as she's the boss, I'd better follow her orders. We'll have dinner when we get back."

Mum got ready, Dad changed into his casual clothes, and we walked down to Grandad's house.

This time, Mum had the garage key so we didn't have to go through the house. That was a shame. I still had my eye on that spear for my bedroom.

She twisted the handle and pushed up the garage door to reveal the dull rusting camper van.

"Well, it's still here," said Mum. "But then, who in their right minds would want to steal it?"

"Don't say things like that, Mum. You could upset it," said Elizabeth.

I grinned at Elizabeth's comment and said, "You know, that would be quite something if it did have feelings and maybe even talk."

"Don't talk nonsense, Danny. This magic thing is getting out of hand."

"It's okay, Mum. I'm just fooling around."

Dad pulled out the van key and got into the driver's seat. He tried to start it, but it made no sound at all.

"The battery must be flat," said Dad.

"Oh, well, since you can't move it, it should stay here, and we forget the lot. I'm more than happy to let others have the responsibility," said Mum.

"It's only the battery, Wendy. We can get it towed to our house and fix it up there. Next door has a Land Rover. I could ask him to help."

"Do you want this rusty old thing that badly, George? The instructions were very clear, 'Don't clean it, don't repair it in any way, don't change it in any way.' Charging the battery may constitute just that!" Mum crossed her arms and looked at Dad.

"It would've been nice to put it into the garage given that Daniel and I worked so hard to make the space," said Dad. "But unless we tow it to the garage or push it, I can't see how we're going to move it."

"George, just leave it for now. Unless it moves itself, we're not going to get it moved to our garage."

Dad looked at the camper van. "Okay, Wendy. I'll have a word with the neighbour about towing it, but I'm beginning to feel just like you, full of questions and no answers. How can we use a camper van to go on holidays when it doesn't work and I can't repair it to make it work?"

We left the van where it was. I felt really sorry for it and for us. I'd hoped that it could lead to some exciting adventures. Elizabeth looked sad so I put my arm around her and gave her a hug. Dad locked the garage doors.

It seemed the only one who was happy about it was Mum, and she had a smirk on her face.

Elizabeth helped Mum with dinner, while I sat in the lounge reading. It was hard to concentrate, and I found myself thinking about the camper van. *What if it did have feelings?*

Chapter Six
A Surprise

Belle and I were sat eating our breakfast in the kitchen when Dad came down, searching for something as usual.

"Bye, kids. Have a great day at school," Dad said as he walked out of the back door and into our garage.

We smiled through our cereal-filled mouths. He was only gone a moment when we heard him shout.

"Wendy. Children. Come in here, quick. You're not going to believe this."

Could it be? Elizabeth and I jumped off our stools and rushed out to the garage.

There in its planned space was Grandad's camper van.

"How did you get that up here, George?" asked Mum as she stepped into the garage.

"That's what I'm saying, Wendy. I didn't. I've just walked in to find it here. I'm as surprised as everyone else."

"Well then, how *did* it get here?"

Both of them fell silent as we all stared at the camper van.

I looked at Belle and she nodded. We were both thinking the same thing. "It must be magic," I said.

"Nonsense, Danny," said Mum. "I'm not going to have any more of this magic rubbish, and that's an end to it. Someone has played a practical joke on us and nothing more. As far as I'm concerned, the person who brought it here can take it right back."

"Well, I can't stay here puzzling about this now," said Dad. "I must get on my way. We can talk about this later."

Dad got into his car, drove out, and gave a wave. Elizabeth and I followed Mum out of the garage.

We finished our preparations for school and put our coats on.

"Go and lock the garage door please, Daniel."

Mum locked the back door, and I went to do as asked.

As I did, I glanced at the camper van, but it wasn't there!

I stood there staring at the *empty* space, and a cold feeling ran down my spine. Was this real? Or was I dreaming?

Mum met me as I stood at the gap, looking along at the space in the other garage.

"Come on, Daniel. Stop gawping at the van and get the door down or we'll be late."

"But, Mum. Look." I pointed to the open space that moments ago had Grandad's camper van in it.

"What on earth is going on? This is turning into a mad house." said Mum. "First it's here, then it's gone. Who's messing about?"

"I have an idea, but you're not going to like it." I wondered how crazy I was going to sound, but it was the only thing that made sense. "I think it's you. You said out loud, 'As far as I'm concerned, the person who brought it here can take it right back,' and that's what happened."

Mum shook her head in disbelief. "You think it's magic?"

"Hang on, Mum," I said. "Last night you said, 'Unless it moves itself, we're not going to get it moved to our garage.' And it did!"

"Well, yes, I vaguely remember saying that. But so what?"

"And this morning, you said, 'the person who brought it here can take it right back.' Last night and this morning, you said those things in front of the van," I said. "I think it listens to you. We all have a share in the inheritance, but it's *you*. You're the catalyst for the van to do magical things."

"No, Daniel. That's enough. I've had enough of this magic rubbish. It's off to school with you and make sure you concentrate on your lessons."

We made our way to school and left Mum at the gate. I was full of queries about the magic camper van as school dragged on. All I had to do was convince Mum that it was a magic vehicle. But how?

At last the school day ended, and as I was about to leave the classroom my teacher said, "Daniel, can you wait a moment until everyone has left? I need to have a word with you."

I waited until the rest of my class had filtered out and stood at her desk.

"What's been going on, Daniel? You've paid very little attention to my lessons all day. Are you feeling ill?"

"I apologise, Mrs Sheppard," I said. "I've been thinking about my Grandad. My mum found him dead in his chair at his home. I just can't get him out of my mind."

It was a lie of sorts, bending the truth, I like to say, but it was to do with Grandad after all!

She smiled and said, "Try not to dwell on it quite so

much. Try to come to terms with the fact that he died in his own home, knowing he was loved by all of the family."

I wouldn't have put it quite like that, but Mum must have had some love for him. And now that love was being returned in the shape of the magic camper van.

She let me go, and I pulled my coat on as I ran to the school doors and out into the front of the school.

Mum was waiting with Elizabeth. "Where have you been?"

"Mrs Sheppard wanted to go over a few points about a lesson today, but there's no problem," I said, not lying but not giving her the whole truth. I didn't want Mum knowing that I'd spent most of my time thinking about the camper van instead of paying attention to lessons. I'd be grounded for a long time if she figured it out!

Mum seemed happy with the answer, and we returned home.

Once inside, Mum said, "Sit down both of you. I have a few things I need to say."

"Now listen, I've been thinking about what you said this morning," Mum said. "I'm not saying you're right. I don't go along with all this mumbo-jumbo, but there are a few things that support the idea that the van has some sort of strange power we don't yet understand."

"So you're coming around to the thought our new van might be magic. Wait until Dad comes home. I think when you tell him this," I said, "he'll need a drink. He'll be just as surprised as I was when the camper van disappeared. And remember he doesn't know you commanded it to go back to Grandad's house!"

"Oh, goodness, you're right." She sank slowly into

the lounge chair. "I hope he won't be bothered by that."

"I shouldn't think so, Mum," said Elizabeth. "Dad will do his usual Dad thing, think about it, and then start asking questions."

"And because of that, you'll be able to tell him we've discovered that the main instruction has got to come from you." Then another thought came to me. "That must've been how it worked for Grandad. You inherited it, and now you're the next Rowland in line to control or use it."

"I feel peculiar. Am I now magic, or is it just the van?"

"I think it's just the van. Now you sit for a little while longer, Mum. I'll get you a drink of water. I don't think any of us are settled with the thought that the van is magic, but how else can we explain it? Relax. Let Dad come home, then we can all talk about it, and decide what to do," I said.

She sipped from the mug of water then said, "Danny, you might have got me a glass to drink from rather than a mug."

She was becoming more at ease now. Amazing what a mug of water can do!

"I must get on with dinner," she said as she rose from the chair. "Will you two go upstairs and finish your homework, please?"

Feeling a lot happier, Elizabeth and I went upstairs and set about finishing our homework before Dad came home. I found I was able to concentrate a lot better.

Once I'd finished, I packed it into my rucksack. I looked at the new stuff I'd been given today but decided I'd done enough.

I went downstairs and reported to Mum, who always liked to know that I was keeping on top of it all.

33

"Daniel, give me a hand and set the table will you please?"

"Of course," I said and started to take out the cutlery.

"I've been thinking about the camper van, and I wondered if Grandad used it to go out for meals."

"Using the van, you mean?" I asked, as I carefully set the knives and forks on the table. Mum liked it to be neat.

"Yes, I suppose I do. Do you think he sent it to any takeaway and drive-through places?"

"I don't think so. He'd need to be in the van to pay." After a few moments, I asked, "Why would you be thinking about takeaway places, Mum?"

"Well, Daniel, Grandad must have used it somehow. I just wondered if he would be able to tell it to go and get his takeaway meals—there were enough empty cartons stacked in the kitchen."

"I think it's more likely he used the phone like we did for our Chinese a few days ago."

"Oh, well, it was just a thought."

Mum carried on with the dinner, and the aroma began to make my stomach rumble.

"I take it all back, Mum. You are magic. That dinner is magic to my eyes."

"I don't think your eyes have anything to do with it, Daniel," said Elizabeth. "I heard your stomach rumble. I bet the whole street heard it and are worried it was an earth quake!"

I laughed at my sister's jibe, as did Mum.

Once we stopped laughing, Mum looked at us and said "I think I should throw another thing into the melting pot."

"We're not talking food here, are we, Mum?" I asked, slightly apprehensively.

"No, we're not. You remember when we first discovered the van, and we all got in it?"

Elizabeth and I nodded.

"Do you remember me saying something about it being a 'little squashed up,' and then it expanded? Well, I think that's something else for us to talk about when your dad comes home."

I grinned. "I knew all along that it was magic."

"And now Mum is beginning to come around to the idea that we've been given something quite amazing," remarked Elizabeth.

Grinning, we gave each other a high five.

Grandad's extraordinary camper van *is* magic.

Chapter Seven
What Next?

My mind was racing with questions. How could we get the camper van to do something different for us? Could it fly? Could it drive itself? Could it change shape and become a racing car? The list of questions was almost endless, and Dad was still nowhere to be seen.

Finally, we heard the garage door close and in he came.

"Did I dream that the camper van was in our garage this morning?" he asked.

"You weren't dreaming, George. It *was* there...but it's most likely back at Grandad's house."

"Did someone move it back there? What's going on?"

Mum nodded. "Someone did, and we believe it was me!"

"You started the van and drove it back to your grandad's garage? Why?"

"Sit down, George, take a deep breath, and listen to me. I said it's most likely back at Grandad's house. I don't know for sure because I didn't start the van's engine, but I may have driven it back to Grandad's garage another way."

Dad sank down into his chair and ran his hand through his hair. "But, Wendy, how can you drive it if you don't know how you drove it there? Did you go back into that plant room? Have you been taking in a little too much la-la air?"

I tried to keep down a laugh. I couldn't look at Elizabeth because I could see her shaking shoulders from the corner of my eye. If we looked at each other, I just know we would've burst out laughing.

"George, I haven't been to the house without you. And I'm not under any form of drug influence nor will I ever be."

Dad held up his arms, clearly frustrated. "Sorry, Wendy, but you're just not making any sense."

"Let me put the vegetables on, and I'll tell you what we think has happened while I finish the dinner."

We all followed Mum into the kitchen and watched her check the pans of vegetables on the stove.

She then continued by saying, "When you went to work, I stood in the garage and said, 'the person who brought it here can take it right back.' When Daniel went to lock the garage door, he saw that the van was gone!"

"Well, that would be about ten minutes at the most, between me leaving and you going with the children."

"Exactly. Wait just a moment while I check the veg again." Mum prodded the steaming vegetables with a fork. "Perfect. Okay, let's have our meal, and I'll tell you our theory when we're done."

"Ramping up the anticipation, are you, Wendy?"

Mum smiled and said nothing more. It was almost as if she were enjoying the mystery. She served up and the food looked amazing. We sat down and tucked in, conversation forgotten for the moment. I wolfed mine down as fast as I could, desperate to hear what Dad would make of all this. Everyone finally finished and we sat in the lounge.

"Okay, Wendy. You have the floor," said Dad.

"Well, in truth, this is mostly the children's idea. They pointed a few things out that got me wondering."

Mum then told Dad what we had said about her giving instructions to the camper van, and how the van seemed to *listen* to her and then do what she'd said. She got to the bit where she'd said the van was cramped.

"Yes, I remember you saying that. And I thought Elizabeth had turned the key or pushed a button."

"My conclusion, George, much as I hate to admit it, is that we've inherited a magical camper van."

"That's quite a leap, but I'm happy to test it. So, Wendy the witch, I think we should all go down to Grandad's house, check that the camper van is there, and then you can command it to return to our garage."

"Shall I get my pointy hat and the broom stick?"

"Perhaps. This could be a latent thing in your side of the family."

"George, if you're not careful, I'll turn you into a frog!"

"You'd kiss me eventually so I've got nothing to worry about. Shall we get our coats and go investigate?"

"Oh yes, please. And Mum, if you are a witch, you're the nicest witch I know," said Elizabeth.

"Thank you, sweetheart," said Mum as we put our coats on.

Mum locked up, and we walked down to Grandad's house. Dad opened the garage door.

There, in the exact same place it had been when we first saw it, was the camper van.

We all stared at it for a moment.

"Now what?" asked Mum.

"We could just stand here and tell it to go back to our home," I said.

"Ooh, can we get in it then?" asked Elizabeth.

"I don't think that's a good idea—not until we know how it works," said Mum.

"Wendy, you're the main factor in this. Now go up to it and tell it to go back to our garage. But do it nicely. We've mucked it about enough."

"You want me to be nice to the camper van? George, you have got to be joking."

"Just do this, please, Wendy. We need it to go to our garage more than ever now. This could be like that film about a Beetle car. That was magic, but it was just a story. *This* is the real thing."

"No laughing—any of you." Mum approached the camper van and touched the door. "I'm really sorry for any trouble I've caused, but it's difficult to accept you're a magic camper van," she said quietly. "Would you mind returning to our garage again, and we'll make you very welcome."

The camper van shook and just vanished!

We all saw it happen, and a cold shiver ran down my spine.

"It really is a magical camper van," I exclaimed.

Mum was still standing looking at the empty space, her hand in the same place the van had been.

"Well, I don't believe it. But I must," said Dad. "I think we need to go back to our house and see if it's there again."

Dad locked the garage, and we made our way up the road to our house with Elizabeth and I running ahead.

We jumped up and down with excitement as our parents arrived, and Dad opened the doors to our garage. The camper van was where it had been this morning.

"Well, if I hadn't seen it with my own eyes, I wouldn't have believed it," said Mum.

"Me either," said Dad.

Elizabeth and I looked at each other. We didn't need to say anything. We *knew* it was magic.

"What next?" asked Dad.

We went back into the house to discuss the camper van and its possibilities.

"How do we use it to travel anywhere?" asked Mum. "We can't just say 'take us to the local shops.' Think what would happen. People seeing it suddenly appearing next to their cars would think aliens had landed. There'd be pandemonium!" said Mum. "And think of Mrs Williams with her heart problems—if she saw it suddenly appear, we'd have one more funeral to go to."

"Goodness, you're right, Wendy. How are we to do this?"

"Grandad managed it somehow," I said.

"That's right, Daniel. We just have to figure out how to use it without causing panic in the people who might see it appear," Dad replied.

"I wonder if it can transport all of us at the same time," I said. "What if it's just Mum?"

"Oh, Grandad, why didn't you leave a book of instructions?" asked Mum.

We sat in silence for a short while, each with their own thoughts. My mind was racing: if it could transport itself up the road, could it go to the moon? Daniel, the space boy, bringing home samples from the moon.

"It's quite dark now. Why don't we all get in, and Mum tells it to park outside of Grandad's house," Elizabeth said.

"Yeah, that's a great idea, Elizabeth," I said.

"Okay. This is the bit that I was dreading. I just hope that when it disassembles me, it remembers what parts go where when it puts me together again."

We laughed but there was a little part of me that thought about breaking up into tiny pieces as we went back to the garage.

Mum looked at the camper van then pulled the kitchen door shut. We all got in the camper van and I noticed Mum shaking like mad. "It's going to be okay, Mum," I said and squeezed her arm gently.

"Ready?" asked Dad as he put the key in the ignition.

Everyone turned to look at Mum.

Silence.

"Mum, you need to tell the camper van where we want to go," I said.

She looked at me then at the rest of us staring at her.

"Take us to Grandad's house and park outside on the street, please."

Nothing happened!

"The door, Dad. We need the door shut," I called out.

Just after the door closed, the camper van began to shake and the garage dissolved as we watched. Moments later, we were parked outside Grandad's house.

Dad tried to open the door but couldn't, and two people walked by us as we sat there. As they disappeared around the corner, the door opened for Dad.

He got out and shut his door, walked around to the door on our side and opened it.

"Well, that's made sense of that. We can't get out

while people are nearby."

"And we didn't change or anything."

"I never felt a thing," said Belle.

"Let's go home," said Mum. "I really feel all at odds with this magic."

Dad shut the door, and as he went to walk back around the camper van to the driver's door, the van shook, the view changed from the road, and we were back in the garage without Dad.

"That was quick," I said. "Dad didn't even have a chance to get in."

"We're learning about this amazing camper van, though. Thankfully, Dad hasn't got far to go to get here. Imagine what it would be like if you stranded him or us in the middle of nowhere," Elizabeth said.

"I wonder if it's just you or if any of us could tell the van what to do," I said.

Mum opened the door and got out just as Dad entered the garage.

"Wendy, you're going to have to be careful what you say and when you say it! The van does what you tell it do immediately!"

Mum opened the house up and went upstairs without a word. I looked at Dad and he shrugged.

"Who knows, Daniel?"

Ten minutes later, she returned.

"I've just checked that I'm still all together and no bits missing. I'm not comfortable about the way we all disappear then reappear."

"Wendy, you didn't disappear; the van did. Did any of the children vanish when you asked the camper van to go to Grandad's house? Everything inside remained the same. It *is* magic—it's the outside that changes and the inside is like a cocoon."

"Well, George, I needed to be sure. You all seem to

be very comfortable with this hocus-pocus stuff, but I'm not so happy about it."

"Mum, it's proved we can all be transported to Grandad's house down the road, and it won't let us out until it feels it's safe for us. That means we can also go to the shops and it'll make sure that we don't disturb the locals as it appears."

Excitement coursed through me. "It also means we can go anywhere. But is that only in England or can we go anywhere in this world, even to space?!"

"Wherever it can go, you just need to make sure that any conversation you're having can't be construed as a command!" said Dad.

"Yes, sorry about that, George."

"Don't worry about it. Daniel makes an interesting point though, one that needs thinking about. But I've had enough testing for one night. Let's clear up and relax for the rest of the evening," Dad said.

He went out, locked the garage doors, and returned.

"Here's to a successful trial run," he said, then went into the lounge to read the paper as Elizabeth and Mum cleared the dishes.

Chapter Eight
Another Testing Time

The next morning, Mum walked us to the school gates as usual.

"I'm off to look into a few things. See you after school!" she said cheerily.

Elizabeth and I waved and went into school.

At the end of school my teacher, Mrs Sheppard, called me over before I left the classroom.

"I'm glad to see that you're back to your usual academic level and our little talk seems to have helped with you coming to terms with your Grandad's death," she said.

I nodded and said, "I'm going to the funeral. After that, I should be okay."

She smiled and let me go, and I caught up with Elizabeth as we met Mum at the gate.

"This way," Mum said and led us around the corner.

As we walked up the road, we saw the camper van.

"Yay! We're going home in the camper van!" I said jumping in the air.

Mum grinned. "Yes, this was one of the things that I wanted to attend to. I told it to park in Rochester Street next to the school. I sat in the driver's seat, and it did it.

It just dissolved itself from our garage and reappeared just parked in the road as you see it."

"Are we going home in it now?" I asked.

"I see no reason to waste good shoe leather when we can just get into the van and be home in a few seconds. I'm getting quite used to it now, and each time I've done it, I've not disintegrated."

"Mum, you said each time you've done it. Have you been practising time travelling while we were in school?"

"Good question, Danny. I missed that."

"Elizabeth, I've told you before, I don't like your names shortened. Please remember this in future."

"Okay, Mum, but you haven't answered Daniel's question."

"I'll answer it all in good time, but not now."

Not a satisfactory answer, but I noticed a little smirk on Mum's face.

I tried the door, but it wouldn't open. I turned to Mum.

She smiled. "We can't have just anybody getting into our special inheritance, can we? I told it to lock all the doors and let no one in until I say so. Watch." She turned to the camper van. "Please unlock the doors now so we can all get in."

I tried the door again and it opened.

"It really is only you that can ask it to do something," said Elizabeth, in what can only be described as a disconsolate voice.

"Well, yes and no. Perhaps I could tell it who else it should listen to. Remember, Grandad Rowland was on his own, and it's got used to one person telling it where to go."

We climbed in as thoughts rushed through my mind. One day I could be telling it to take us to the moon. "Well, Mum, I volunteer to be your guinea pig. Why don't you tell it that I'll command it to take us home?"

"Via where? No, I think that test can wait for the moment, Daniel," she said.

"Oh, Mum, it was such a good idea," I said. I was a little disappointed that Mum was so quick to shoot me down in flames.

Once inside the van, Mum in the driver's seat and us in the back.

"Return us to our garage, please," Mum said.

The camper van shook and as the view outside dissolved, so the inside of our garage appeared.

"Quite remarkable, isn't it?" asked Mum.

"It's amazing," I said.

"I love it," said Belle as she bounced on her seat.

Our astonishing mother was becoming quite the time traveller!

We got out of the camper van and went into the house.

"Mum, are you okay now about our camper van having magic powers," I asked.

"Yes, I think I am now. I just needed time to come to terms with so much power being available to me."

"I'm so glad Grandad Rowland was telling the truth; he did go on holidays. Are we going to try somewhere further afield to see if it's just as easy?" I asked, more in hope than certainty. Mum was only just getting used to it and I didn't want to push her too much, even though I couldn't wait to see what this wonderful van could do.

"I thought we could eat out this evening, and I've found a very nice restaurant online that I'd heard about through the WI. I think it's *time* to celebrate."

"Do we need to book or is it a walk-in sort of

place?" I asked.

"Oh, I've booked a table for four, and I've checked the parking situation."

"Mum, this is great! I can't wait."

"Good. Now go upstairs and do your homework. When your dad gets home, we'll leave for the restaurant. Oh, and change into something more relaxing and casual."

We went upstairs, and then both of us sat on my bed for a pow wow.

"Well, this is a bit of a shock, Belle. We walk to school with a mother who's not sure she can cope with the camper van being magic, and now she's a lot more confident about it. Did you notice how she avoided answering my question. I wonder if something else happened today while we were at school?"

"That's an interesting question, big brother, and I have a feeling the answer will arrive very soon."

Belle pushed herself off my bed.

"I'm going to change before doing any homework," she said and left my room.

Once I'd changed into my favourite jeans and top, I settled down to my homework. Maths is a subject I like.

It didn't feel like long at all before Mum called out that Dad was home.

"Finish up your homework and come join us, kids."

Elizabeth and I went downstairs and joined Mum and Dad in the lounge.

"How about this then? Your mum has booked a restaurant for a special meal, and it involves a little travelling. It's exciting, isn't it?"

"Yeah, it's got me intrigued. How far away is this restaurant then, Mum?" I asked.

"Not far," she said with a wink. She made her way to the internal garage door. "Are you ready?"

Mum told the camper van to unlock its doors, and then told us to get in.

"I like the fact that we don't need seat belts. And I love that we'll arrive almost as soon as we leave. It takes all the pain out of travelling," said Mum. "I think we're ready now. Take us to The View please, Nifty," she said.

The garage dissolved as the van shook and then we were parked on a slight hill.

Mum turned to us. "We're in Newquay, Cornwall. I've been told so many times about this place and thought I would never get the chance to try it. Now I can."

"Cornwall! Are you joking? From Gloucestershire to here in a few seconds?"

"No, Elizabeth, it's no joke. I looked it up online to make sure it was special enough for this occasion. Danny said that we might be able to go anywhere in England, and I thought it was worth a try. You see, I decided that if I was going to be the person who was responsible for the commands, then I had to be positive and come to an understanding with Nifty."

"That's the second time you've said 'Nifty,' Wendy. What's that all about?" asked Dad as he pulled the key from the ignition.

It seemed useless to me, but I suppose it made sense to at least look like our magical camper van needed a key.

"I don't like saying camper van all the time. I gave it some thought and decided I'd call it Nifty because I think it's pretty nifty having a magical mode of transport."

"Are you sure you are the Wendy I kissed goodbye to this morning? You sound like a totally different woman."

"It's the power, Dad," I said. "It's gone to her head now she's a witch." Dad and Belle laughed.

"Are you all going to sit here talking or are we going for a meal in this restaurant?"

"Out you both get," said Dad as he turned to us.

We walked down the slope and soon came across the restaurant. Mum led the way, and we followed along behind.

"I have a table for four under Mrs Short," Mum said to a man near the entrance.

"Wonderful. If you'd like to follow me?" he asked, and he led us to a table with a great sea view.

"Now, everyone, I want to tell you that Grandad Rowland left us quite a large amount of money, so I thought we could celebrate our good fortune by having a meal together to say thank you to him."

"And you've always fancied having a meal in this place since the WI recommended it," Dad said and then smiled at Mum.

Mum grinned. "Well, I can't deny that."

"What a lovely view. It's wonderful to have this to look at while we're eating," said Dad.

I peered through the glass to see we were on the top of the cliffs. I looked down and saw the waves crashing against the rocks. I pulled Belle in to have a look but she shied away.

"That's a bit scary, Danny," Elizabeth said.

"Don't worry, Sis. I'll keep you safe," I said.

Belle gave me a big smile and a hug before going back to her menu.

"What can we have? I've never seen a menu like this before," I said.

"They're under difference courses, Daniel. You've got salads you could have as a starter. Then there are main courses and side dishes."

"Wow, Mum. How do you know so much when you've never been here before?" I asked.

"Good question, Daniel," said Dad.

"I came down with Nifty after taking the children to school," said Mum. "And I asked all about the menu!"

"My time traveller wife has been here before. Whatever next?"

"Then you have the puddings," said Mum, ignoring Dad. "But you don't have to worry because I've already chosen a set meal for all of us with lots of new things we can all try."

"I've ordered some wine for us, George, as we won't be driving back. Our personal driver, Nifty, will take care of that."

Dad gave a big smile and watched as the waiter poured the wine for both of them.

"We'd better just have the one glass, Wendy. We may not be driving home, but I'd be happier observing the law about drink-driving."

"You're right, George. We can take the rest of the bottle home and have it another day."

It was a very nice meal, rather posh, and Mum beamed happily. Now she'd be able to say to her ladies in the WI she'd tried it, and it was just as great as they said it was.

Mum settled the bill, and we wandered back to Nifty.

Once inside Nifty, we returned home, a very happy family. It seemed like we all thought Mum's choice of name for the camper van was very good and the same went for our first great adventure.

What an evening! And what a surprise! Now Mum had fully embraced our magical camper van, I was certain there was more to come.

Chapter Nine
About A Funeral

I woke the next day having had trouble sleeping. *We had a vehicle that could do almost anything!* The possibilities raced through my mind all night.

I guess the rest of the world was sad because they didn't have a magical camper van, for it was a dark, rainy morning. There was the usual bustle but it was slightly muted. I thought about what Mrs Sheppard had said and it dawned on me what everyone must be feeling.

"I think we're all feeling guilty about being so happy with the gift of Nifty when I guess we should be feeling sad. I wonder if he'd understand our euphoria, wherever he is," I said. "I hope so because I wouldn't want him to think we don't care about him."

Mum nodded. "I think you're right, Danny. But Grandad's funeral is tomorrow, and you can tell him how you feel then. Let's focus on school and not think about future plans for the moment. I'll go to the funeral parlour and say a few words to Grandad Rowland. I think that will make us all feel better."

I smiled. Mum was right, as usual. I'd think about what I wanted to say to him. "Are we going to school in Nifty?" I asked.

"If it's still raining, yes. But otherwise we'll walk."

"Say a word of thanks from all of us, Wendy," said Dad. He kissed Mum's forehead. "Bye, kids."

Elizabeth and I said good-bye. We finished our breakfast, rushed to get ready then left for school. The rain had stopped so it looked like we were walking to school.

It seemed that even the weather didn't want us riding in Nifty.

Mum left us at the gate and went on her way, her umbrella up as the rain returned.

In my afternoon history lesson, we had a lecture on the tin mines of Cornwall and the need of the industries for tin and copper to make bronze. Wouldn't it be great if Nifty could go back in time to Cornwall and bring life to this lesson? We then went through sections of the industrial revolution. All very interesting stuff, and the lesson flew by. Lessons ended, and she gave us new homework.

Mum was waiting outside the gate with a big umbrella, and we walked around the corner to find Nifty parked in the same place.

"In you get," said Mum.

We got in as fast as we could to escape the rain.

"Take us home please, Nifty," said Mum.

Nifty gave its usual shudder, and we were in our garage.

As we got out, I noticed that the rain hadn't stayed on the camper van. It seemed to be draining away, and even the puddles from the van were disappearing. Soon, Nifty was dry and not a drop of water could be seen on it.

"It seems that Nifty can dry itself quicker than I can after a shower. That was really strange to watch," I said.

"It really is a remarkable gift," said Mum, and she

gave it a pat on the bonnet before going inside.

"Did you go down to speak to Grandad, Mum?" I asked.

"I did. The funeral director was very helpful and allowed me time to sit with Grandad on my own. I spoke to Grandad. That might sound silly, I know, but I felt that somehow he might be listening. I told him we'd found the van, and it was in our garage."

"It's not silly, Mum. A girl at school said her father had died, and she said she still talks to him. She said it made her feel better."

"That's nice, Danny. I do feel better for hearing that."

"Now about tomorrow. A car will collect us tomorrow at 10.30 a.m. and take us to the crematorium for the service. I don't know of anyone else going but we'll all be there. I've spoken to your head teacher, and you won't be going to school tomorrow."

"How long does a funeral take, Mum?"

"Usually about half an hour. Then we'll come home. It's sad that he has no friends coming, but he led a solitary life by choice. I kept visiting him because I felt no one should be on their own. I did think he put up with my continued visits, but clearly it meant something to him," said Mum. "Anyway, upstairs now, please. You have homework to do, and I have the dinner to prepare."

"Okay, Mum," said Elizabeth.

And we left her to do her magic in the kitchen and went up to start the homework. I did some English but my mind wandered to the funeral tomorrow. This would be my first experience of a funeral, and I wasn't looking forward to it. I'd heard that they burned people in this place—would we have to watch that? We'd seen a film about India and they had a cremation in that, and you could see the body on the fire! I must ask if it's going to be like that, because I didn't like the idea of watching them burn someone.

Dad came home, and Mum called out for us to come downstairs.

"As it's been a cold, wet day, I decided to cook my sausage stew. It should warm everyone from the inside out."

Dad and Elizabeth sat, while I helped Mum with serving of plates because it was my turn. I took everyone's plates to the table, then went back to the kitchen and poured water into the pans to soak them ready for washing up.

After we'd eaten Mum's amazing stew, we all went into the lounge.

"Your grandad made all the arrangements for his funeral. There will be nothing frightening at the service. Mum even says there'll be no singing, just a few words Grandad wrote about his travels."

"He didn't want flowers, either. He said to Mr Adams, 'Just get it done with the least amount of fuss,'" said Mum.

That seemed a shame. I knew how much Mum loved getting flowers from Dad. Didn't everyone love flowers? And Dad had said "No wake," whatever that was. "Are we going to watch them burn Grandad?" I asked, a little spooked out by the thought.

"No, Daniel, nothing like that. Grandad's coffin will go behind a curtained area, and you won't see anything."

"Oh, that's okay, then," I said. *Thank Goodness for that.*

"When the funeral's over, we can concentrate on getting the house cleared. Then we can start thinking about how to travel with the aid of Nifty," said Dad.

"There's an auction house in Leominster. I've asked them to call to see some of the things in the house and to tell us if they have any great value," Mum said.

Please don't let them take the spear.

"I've already arranged for a garden centre to take the plants away. Once we've cleared the house, we can sell it," said Dad.

"The pots are huge Dad. How are they going to get them out?"

"I have no idea, Daniel, but if they don't want them, then I guess it'll be down to the men of the house to remove them!"

"Let's hope they want them then, Dad. That'd be one heavy job."

"You're so right, Daniel. Now I think you should get on with your chores."

"Are you taking me to the community centre, Dad? It's the next rehearsal for our play," said Elizabeth.

"Of course. I hadn't forgotten, Elizabeth," Dad replied. "And I'll be in the car park to pick you up."

"Thanks, Dad."

When Belle returned from her rehearsal, she stopped at my bedroom.

"It's still chucking it down outside Danny," she said. "I hope it's a better day tomorrow...for the funeral."

"Yeah, me too, Belle. It's going to be weird with just the four of us."

"That's sad. I don't know what I'd do without you and all my friends."

I got up and pulled her into a big hug. "Lucky you won't ever have to."

"Night, big bro."

"Night, little miss."

I went down to the lounge, said night to Mum and Dad, and returned to my room. I brushed my teeth and climbed into bed.

I found myself wishing that tomorrow was already over.

Chapter Ten
Good-bye, Grandad Rowland

I didn't remember much of the night. I slept quite well, but when Mum knocked on my door to wake me, it seemed as if I'd only just got in bed.

"Just to remind you, no school today. But I do want you in the shower and dressed as soon as you can. Come down for breakfast when you're ready."

As if I could forget what today was. I headed to the bathroom to stake my claim. When I emerged, Elizabeth was already waiting outside the door.

"Big day," I said.

"I'm dreading it, Daniel," Elizabeth replied.

"It'll be okay, little sis. I promise."

She nodded and closed the bathroom door. It didn't take long before I was downstairs and in the kitchen.

Mum looked at me and raised her eyebrows. I knew that meant trouble.

"Daniel, you're going to a funeral, not a disco. Go up and change into your dark trousers and white shirt and put your school tie on. And get that dark jacket out to go with it."

I didn't argue. She wouldn't change her mind so it'd be a waste of time. I just went back up and changed my clothes.

Elizabeth was downstairs by the time I returned. She was in her dark brown dress and black tights. I wondered if she chose her own outfit or Mum had picked it last night. Mum hadn't said that I had to be dressed in school clothes. Who was going to see us? Grandad wouldn't, even if he was there. I guess I was being a bit sulky being nervous about the funeral, even after Dad's reassurance.

We ate breakfast, cleared the dishes, and sat waiting, playing on our iPads.

Two cars arrived; one with Grandad's coffin in front and one behind it. Dad locked up and we all got in the second car without much conversation.

The first car drove very slowly, just like I'd seen other funeral cars do. I'd once asked Mum why and she'd told me that it gave people time to be close to their loved ones for the last time. It didn't really make sense to me then, but now I was in one, it really did feel right.

When we got to the crematorium, we waited until someone asked us to go in, and the men in the first car with the coffin carried Grandad Rowland into the service room. We followed as they placed it on a stand.

I looked around all the men and one lady that had come with the coffin stood at the back. They outnumbered us, and I was hit with a pang of sadness. I couldn't believe he didn't have any other friends who'd want to say good-bye one last time.

The service was short. A few things were read out about his travels and his favourite piece of music was played. I didn't know he even liked music, let alone had a favourite piece. I guess there was a lot I didn't know about Grandad. I felt my eyes burning a little and took a deep breath to hold back the tears.

They drew some curtains around Grandad's coffin. Mum nudged me gently.

"That's the end of the service, Daniel. Time to go," she said.

I felt quite relieved, and wondered why I'd got so worked up about it.

We got up and moved out through another door. Then Mum thanked the man who had said and read the things about Grandad, and we returned to the car.

It was all over, but quite sad. We were the only ones there to say good-bye. I tried to wipe my eyes without anyone seeing, but when I glanced at Elizabeth, I saw she was doing the same.

We got back in the car and the driver took us home.

"I think a toast to Grandad Rowland is in order, and I think, as Daniel and Elizabeth conducted themselves so well, they should have a drop to join us."

That usually only happened at Christmas, so we beamed at Dad, who got out a bottle of red wine. He poured a small amount in each of our glasses, then a full glass for Mum and himself.

"Remember what I told you; drink slowly and enjoy it. Take your glasses and drink to Grandad Rowland. Safe journey."

He drank from his glass, as did we. Dad's choice of words seemed strange to me. Where was he journeying to?

Chapter Eleven
A Few Surprises

On Saturday, Mum had decided that we'd concentrate on clearing Grandad's place.

After breakfast, we all walked down to the house. It was very overcast but not raining. We arrived at the house and as Dad opened the door, a small pile of letters was pushed back.

Dad picked up the letters and passed some to Mum. He sat in Grandad's chair, as Mum sat in the other.

"This is interesting," said Dad as he read the letter. "It's from an auction house asking if Grandad would like to put any items in their auction next month."

"Perhaps that's how he made a bit of money to travel with," I said.

"More than a little bit," said Mum. "I closed his account with amounts numbered in thousands!"

"Maybe we should be asking about the pocket money increase again," I said.

"You can be summed up by two things Daniel: food and money," said Mum.

"And not necessarily in that order," said Belle, laughing.

Mum went on, "It says to ring again if he wants someone to do an appraisal and arrange carriage to the auction rooms."

"I've already contacted the Leominster auction house, and they're sending someone called Mr Curtis today around ten. If he doesn't want the things, we could always contact them instead."

"Sounds like a plan, Wendy," said Dad. He smiled and gave the letter to her.

Mum finished the rest of the letters and put them in a pile.

The doorbell rang, and Dad went out to answer it. I heard him talking to someone, and he returned with another man.

"This is Mr James. He's here to see the plants."

Dad led him into the back room as we started sorting out the items in boxes in the corner of the room. Elizabeth and I helped take out the wrapped items very carefully. It was my job to unwrap the newspaper and pass it to Elizabeth.

I found lots of figurines and unusual shaped vases of many colours.

"Oh, that's lovely," Mum said as she looked at one. "I think I'll keep that."

Mum had a pad of paper, and she wrote what the item was and where it was made before she gave it to Elizabeth to rewrap with the item in the paper.

Strangely, though I'd thought it was going to be really boring, I found the job interesting. It felt like I was doing something to help Grandad. And with the system we had, the pile of boxes was soon catalogued and restacked.

Next was the bigger stuff, and I still had my heart set on the spear. I picked it up, but Mum shook her head.

"Leave that until Dad's available," said Mum. "I don't want any accidents."

Would the spear never be mine?!

A few minutes later Dad came in. "Mr James is very impressed with the condition of the plants and couldn't believe they were inside a house. He says Grandad must've been an expert gardener for them to thrive that way. He'd like to have all of the plants, but he needs a crew of men to handle the bigger plants and a flatbed truck to load them on—they're going to be very heavy to move. If we're happy to let him come back this afternoon, he could clear the room."

"Well, that's good news. Has he gone now?"

"Not yet. He wants to know if seven hundred pounds would be enough, so I said I'd come and ask you."

"Oh, well it seems a lot to ask, but yes, pay the man, George. Let's get rid of them as soon as we can."

"No, Wendy. He wants to pay us that! Some of these plants are very expensive, and he can sell them quite easily."

I looked at Mum who was sat with her mouth open looking at Dad in amazement.

"I'll take your look as a yes," said Dad and went back to the Greenhouse room next door.

He wasn't gone long before he escorted the plant man out and came back to help us with the stuffed animal heads, birds, and butterflies.

Dad picked up an evil-looking stone head thing.

"This is a gargoyle, kids," Dad said. "It was an old-fashioned way of getting rid of water on churches or other buildings."

Whatever they were, I didn't want one in my bedroom like I wanted that spear. Behind the settee, we found three different ones about the same size.

Mum made a list and soon we came to an end of items in the room.

The doorbell rang, and Dad answered it. He came in with another man that Mum seemed to know. He had a face a bit like one of the gargoyles!

"Thank you for coming, Mr Curtis. We've been going through the things. Elizabeth has taken a photo of each item we've found. And I've made a note on each item to show you."

He sat down and spent some time flicking through Elizabeth's photos and looking at Mum's notes.

"You've got a lot of items here that will fetch a good price, Mrs Short. The pair of Staffordshire figurines could fetch a really high sum. All four figures are highly collectable and should fetch two to three hundred pounds each."

"Goodness me! What a surprise!" exclaimed Mum.

"I'd be very happy to put these items in my next auction. If you're happy to let me value everything, I can arrange to collect everything this afternoon, if that's convenient?"

"Oh, yes, that would be most helpful," said Mum, sounding more excited by the minute. "That should give us time to sort out one of the other rooms before you come. I think there'll be other things going you might want in there."

Dad showed the auction guy to the door, and I looked at Mum who was doing a good impression of a goldfish with her mouth open.

"How amazing. I wasn't expecting that," she finally said.

"It's great," I said. "Let's go upstairs and see what we can find there!" I led the way into one of the bedrooms at the front of the house. Dad lifted a box down, and we opened it to find it was filled with children's toys; a train set in a box and a box of Meccano, a kind of building set to make a crane.

"Wow, aren't these great?" asked Dad.

I scrunched my nose, not at all impressed. Give me an iPad any day!

Dad took it downstairs after Elizabeth had taken some photographs and Mum had made notes. We worked our way through the boxes, taking them downstairs, and stacking them in the front room.

Gargoyle guy was going to get quite a surprise at all the extra things we found, like the Titanic lifebelt, the fancy Royal plates, big jugs with faces on them, tribal masks and seven full sized flags from other countries.

We went home for lunch, tired and dirty from all of the dust. I was halfway through my sandwich when a big lorry went past our house.

"I think that was the plant truck," said Dad.

"Let me wrap your sandwich and we'll join you in a little while," said Mum.

By the time we'd finished and had walked down to Grandad's house, a lot of his big plants were wrapped in big bags and tied onto the bed of the lorry. The men were going in and out of the house at quite a pace and were coming out with large boxes. I could see the smaller plants peeking out of the air holes.

"Is it okay to pay you cash?"

"Yes, of course it is, Mr James."

He pulled out a mega wallet, stuffed with money, and counted out the money. He then asked Mum to sign a receipt to say she'd been paid and gave her a copy. He shook Mum's hand and they left with the plants blowing in the wind.

We went into the plant room and looked at the now empty room that once had the plants. The floor covering was still there but everything else had gone. Mum went across to the windows, pulled down the thick paper that was stuck to the glass, and light flooded in. I noticed mould marks on the walls and figured that must be where the funny smell was coming from.

"Back up to the bedrooms?" I asked.

"You're good at keeping us on track, Danny," said Dad with a smile.

We finished the boxes in the one started, then went into the bedroom that had been Grandad's bedroom. It felt a bit weird, knowing that Grandad would never sleep in his bed again, but I tried not to think about it. A few boxes of items were on the floor, but this room had just the wardrobe, a chest of drawers, and the bed. Mum pulled out the clothes from the wardrobe one by one and went through the pockets before folding them and putting them into some big black bags.

"This will all be wonderful for the charity shop," she explained.

Once this was done, we went into the box room. Piles of newspapers and old books were stacked on the floor. I noticed an old Dandy album among them. "That could be worth something too, Mum," I said.

"Well, let's box it up and see if Mr Curtis agrees with you, Daniel." She took it from me and passed it to Elizabeth. "How about you get the profits of the sale if he wants it?"

"That'd be awesome, Mum!"

"And we'll find something to do the same for you, Elizabeth," Mum said.

She must've read Belle's mind, because she looked like she was just about to complain about not having something!

We went back downstairs just as another big van arrived.

"It's the gargoyle guy," I whispered to Belle and she giggled. Dad opened the door and he came in with the two other men.

"Make sure you put the heavy boxes in first." He pointed to the boxes. "And what about that spear, Mr Short?"

I looked at Dad and said, "Please can I keep the spear, Dad? It would look great in my bedroom, and I'd always have a reminder of Grandad and his prickly personality."

Dad smiled. "I'm not sure, Daniel. It's a dangerous weapon." He took the spear and ran his finger over the end of it. "Though it's not that sharp...What do you think, Wendy? Is our boy old enough to be trusted with something like this?"

Mum came over and inspected the spear. "Do you promise to be careful with it?" she asked.

I nodded. "Absolutely. I promise, promise, promise."

"That's a triple promise, Daniel. You can't break those," said Dad.

"I won't." Was it finally going to be mine?

Mum and Dad looked at each other, then at the spear, then back at me. I could barely handle the anticipation! They shared a little nod, then Dad handed it to me.

"Put it somewhere safe, and remember that it's not a toy," Dad said.

I took it from him as if it were the most precious thing in the world. "I will." Yes! I couldn't wait to put it in my room, but I placed it out of the way of the moving guys and watched them go to work.

Now I knew first-hand about house clearance. After almost an hour, everything was gone and just a few chairs and side cupboards remained.

"Well, that was a good day's work," said Mum.

"Most charity shops need furniture," said Dad. "Maybe one would like to collect all of this, then the house is ready to be cleaned, ready to sell."

Dad and I found a bucket and a shovel, and we went into the ex-plant room. Mum pulled the waste bin to the front of the house and then she and Elizabeth would go home to make dinner.

I filled the bucket, and Dad took it out. Soon we had most of it done. We lifted the heavy black underlay from the floor, folded it up and took it out. Once the last strip was lifted, we pulled the bin down to the front driveway gate and parked it ready for collection.

"Come on, Danny, I think we've done enough for today. Time to close up the house and go home."

Dad locked up. I passed him the spear, and we walked home.

Mum was in her dressing gown. "Elizabeth is in the shower. You go and clean up next before dinner," she said.

"We'll leave this here for now, Danny." Dad put the spear against the wall. "You can put it in your room later."

"Okay, Dad."

We all sat around after our meal in our pyjamas. I was exhausted...but at least I had my spear to show for all my hard work!

Chapter Twelve
Messing About on the River

I woke to the sound of rain falling against our windows and the occasional rumble of thunder in the distance.

I pulled my dressing gown on and ambled downstairs.

Dad, still in his pyjamas, was sat reading a damp newspaper. Our neighbour picked one up for Dad when he went to the local shop.

Mum was already dressed and ready for action. "Good morning, Daniel. Are you wanting a cup of tea to help wake up?"

"Thanks, Mum," I said and sat on the island stool waiting, supporting my head in case it fell off! I'm not a morning person.

Elizabeth came into the kitchen and looked at me. "Danny is his usual, bright self then."

I poked my tongue out at her, and she laughed.

Mum smiled. "Well, the ladies of the house have got dressed, but the men are still just thinking about it."

I yawned, drank the last of my tea, and went upstairs to wash my face in the hope it might wake me up a little. I felt much better as I got dressed. I returned to the kitchen to find another cup of tea waiting for me and decided that I might live after all!

"What's the order of the day today then, Mum?"

"I've looked at the weather, and we're going to have rain most of the day but they have sunshine up north. I thought a trip to Cumbria might be nice. We could have a picnic and if Nifty's little cooker top works, we could even have some warm food."

Dad put down his newspaper suddenly. Usually nothing got his nose out of the paper first thing in the morning.

"I'm going up to get dressed. I don't want to miss out on this test drive," he said and went upstairs.

"Can you go online and find us a place to start, Daniel?" asked Mum. "Then we can decide if we want to go to other places when we get there. I've never been up there before but some ladies in the WI tell me it's beautiful."

We wandered into the lounge and I sat down at the family computer. "It's the Lake District area, Mum," I replied after a quick search. "There's Lake Windermere for a start. It says that Kendal and Ambleside are the most popular towns. Ambleside is at the point of the lake, and Kendal is a little way from it. They've got lovely looking towns and old brick buildings. One of my friends at school went there for a holiday last summer. He said it was really busy so parking might be a problem."

"Let's leave that to Nifty," she said.

Dad came into the lounge. "I'd like to go to Ambleside. I went camping there as a lad with the scouts a long time ago."

"Excellent. That's one of the places Daniel found. Let's visit that and Kendal," Mum said.

"Sounds lovely. Are we going to eat out or are you doing something in Nifty?"

"We could eat out, but let's just go on an

adventure," said Mum. "We can take tea, coffee, and milk. We don't know if the kitchen works yet, but it looks new so we should be able to boil the kettle for a cup of tea."

"A picnic it is then," said Dad.

"Now I'll make up a quick salad and bag up a few cold meats, and we should be ready," said Mum.

"Right," said Dad. "Get your cameras, a warm coat in case it gets cold, wellingtons in case it's mucky, and any other bits you might need."

Belle and I rushed upstairs excitedly, leaving Mum and Dad downstairs sorting out things for our picnic type stop if it was possible.

Loaded with our oddments, we went out to the garage and put everything in Nifty. Mum came out with a bag full of food and gave it to me to put in the cupboard under the cooking area.

Once we were packed, we all got in and waited for Mum to give the order!

"We'd like to go to Kendal please, Nifty," said Mum.

Nifty shook and we were there!

"This is a much nicer way to travel long distances," I said. No matter how much I loved my sister, she was still terrifically annoying in the back of the car for hours.

"I know exactly what you mean, Daniel," said Dad. He got out and looked at the parking sign. "Looks like we've got two hours free parking. We better get a wriggle on."

We got out and wandered down into the town.

It was just like I'd seen on the internet; quaint stone-built houses and shops, little lanes and cobbled roads. It was like something from another time. Looking up one small lane, we saw a house built with a walkway underneath it but not big enough for a car to go under.

We wandered into the market square and then down to the river. A bridge spanned the river, and we could see a small waterfall from it. Dad reminded us that it was called a weir.

As a treat for us all, Mum bought some Kendal Mint cake. This was almost like the bars of chocolate we could get in the sweet shops but bigger and really nice to try. I found it a little too sweet, so saved half of it, as did Mum. Dad and Belle finished theirs.

The time passed quickly, and we returned to our parking space to get in Nifty and to leave before the two hours were up.

"It's a pity we can't drive to Ambleside like a normal car would. It'd be nice to see some of the countryside."

Nifty shook a little, then pulled out onto the road and began to drive!

Dad tried to take over the steering, but he jumped back when he touched the wheel.

"Nifty doesn't want me to drive," he said. "Bloody thing just gave me an electric shock!"

"Don't swear in front of the children, George," Mum said.

Belle and I giggled and sat back to enjoy the ride.

"Nifty's taking us on the countryside route, just like you asked, Mum. Now you can relax and enjoy the view."

"Mmm." Dad grumbled. "It seems to know what it's doing, I suppose."

"Me and my big mouth. Is there nothing that this vehicle can't do?" muttered Mum.

I leaned to the side and could see she was still hanging onto the door handle tight enough to make her knuckles white!

We made our way to Ambleside at the edge of the lake. Nifty parked in a space after another car had just vacated.

Mum looked very relieved. "I need the loo. That was quite a shock!"

We all got out and walked back down further into the town.

Mum returned having made herself comfortable, and we all continued our exploration of the town.

Ambleside was much the same as Kendal. It had stone houses and was really quaint. A river came down through the town, and I saw a house built on a bridge.

"Wow, that must've taken some doing," I said.

"A house on a bridge," Mum said. "That's nothing compared to our Nifty."

She had a point! We wandered in and out of shops, and it was lovely to just enjoy the experience. The two hours were nearly up as we drifted back to Nifty.

"I'm hungry. Let's have our picnic," Mum said and climbed into the back of the van.

Elizabeth and I sat at the back to give her more room. She opened the bag I'd stored for her and began to sort lunch.

"Oh, dear, this is so squashed up. Would you give me more room to move about, Nifty?" Nifty shook and expanded, just as it had before. "Now, what else could we do with?"

"It would've been nice to have eaten in one of those boats as it took us around the lake," said Dad. "Imagine the views from that as we sat eating our picnic."

"That sounds lovely, I would've liked that. But we couldn't leave Nifty here and risk a parking ticket."

Nifty began to shake and suddenly we had a view of the lake...because we were on the lake!

"Mum, look," I called out. "You said the picnic on the lake would be nice and now Nifty is a boat. And quite a big one by the looks of it."

Mum dropped bag she was holding and grabbed for the sink to hold on to. "George, is it safe? This is a road vehicle, not a boat. Are we all going to drown?"

"I don't think so, Wendy. This van is remarkable and seems to be able to do anything you ask. Let go of the sink, relax, and enjoy the view."

Mum gave Dad one of her looks then carefully made her way to the front, looking around at the floor as if expecting water to come in at any moment.

Elizabeth and I were not wholly convinced once

Mum had said this. We both looked at each other then down to the floor. No water was in evidence, so I felt a little happier and I guess so did Elizabeth.

Dad took her hand. "We're cruising along the lake, just like those other boats. Nifty's even created a walkway and a deck so we can go outside."

Dad went to open the driver's door, but Mum was having none of it.

"Don't open it, George. I'm not convinced about the ability of this van to float!"

Dad smiled at her, opened it, and stepped out. "Come on, Wendy. It's what you wished for us. Have faith in our wonderful little Nifty."

Mum followed, looking a little unsure, and stepped out to join Dad.

Still a little surprised and amazed we were not sinking, I followed Belle and joined Mum and Dad.

"Now, isn't this nice?" asked Dad. "Our own personal boat skippered by captain Nifty. Look over the edge; the wheels and tyres are hanging on the side to stop any damage should we dock."

Elizabeth and I took a quick peek at what Dad was talking about, before we wandered around the deck, keen to explore. We found a larger space at the rear of our super van-boat.

"Can we sit here and have our picnic, Mum?" Elizabeth called out.

Mum soon appeared behind us. "I suppose so if we're careful. It's a bit small. A table would be nice," Mum said. "I'm just in total shock at all this. It's hard to come to terms with this magic business. Each time I open my mouth and something like this happens, it scares me a little."

Nifty shook. The rear of the boat extended and a table unfolded from the floor.

"You see, it's done it again! Oh, well, let's get the picnic set up here then."

"We'll help, Mum," said Elizabeth.

"You stay here and enjoy the sunshine, Daniel. We'll hand things out to you."

I grinned. Mum must've figured out I just wanted to relax.

As we all sorted the picnic, I could see Dad sat at the front watching the boats in front of us. Once everything was laid out, I called him to join us.

He came to the back of our super van-boat and sat down. "We're slowly catching up to the boat in front, but Nifty seems to be keeping its eyes on it...or should I say, lamps?"

Elizabeth and I giggled, and even Mum laughed. She seemed to be coming around to the idea of our fabulous camper van floating on water.

We had a lovely time eating Mum's tasty picnic and watching the scenery go by. After we'd finished, I cleared the plates and took them inside to the sink.

As I walked to the door, we started to overtake the other boat.

People on it waved, and we waved back. Soon it was behind us.

"I'm leaving the dishes," Mum said. "I'm just going to sit for a while and relax, then we can decide what we want to do next." Mum sat in a chair, looking out from the rear of our van-boat. "This really is a lovely day."

Within five minutes, I could see she'd fallen asleep.

"Can we go to the front to watch the other boats, Dad?" I asked.

Dad put his finger to his mouth to indicate we should be quiet and let Mum sleep. We all moved to the front with our chairs. We watched the other boats come and go; some people looked at our strange boat while others barely glanced at us.

After half an hour, Mum came to the front.

"I was so content, I dropped off to sleep."

"You must've needed it, Wendy. It's nice to see you relax," said Dad.

She smiled. "Well, if everyone is ready, I think I'd like to get back on dry land. It's getting cold, and there's a big black cloud coming up behind us."

"It's been a lovely day, Nifty, but would you take us home now?" asked Mum.

Our super van-boat shook and we were back in our garage in an instant.

I got out to see that Nifty changed back to the camper van we knew and were very much beginning to love. "There's water leaking from Nifty," I said.

"Well, it has been on a lake. We have to expect a little seepage."

We all laughed.

I ran my hand along Nifty's bonnet. "Thanks, Nifty."

Chapter Thirteen
A Letter from the Past

We all woke the next day to our usual Monday pattern. Elizabeth and I were on countdown to the school holidays—two more weeks until the big break.

Dad was eating his scrambled eggs on toast, his regular Monday breakfast.

I grabbed myself some cereal and Mum gave me a cup of tea. I sat down and greeted Elizabeth as she came in.

The day was overcast but not raining. It didn't matter what the weather was doing—nothing would dampen my spirit after our day out yesterday.

"I had a wonderful day yesterday, Mum. How about you?"

"I did. It's nice of you to ask, Daniel," said Mum. "I've been thinking about yesterday quite a lot. If I'm going to wish for something, I should really think about the practicalities before I speak. I could've said a submarine, and we might have been drowned. So, no more trips until I get my mind on just how Nifty can be used. Now concentrate in your lessons, and I'll see you after school."

"I think Nifty's proved that's not how it works.

I don't think it'd try to do something it couldn't, do you?" I replied. Nifty was all right in my book. "And isn't the only way to see what it can do is to ask it?"

Mum patted me on the shoulder and gave me a gentle push toward the school gate.

"Maybe, Daniel. Off you go."

We went in to school, and my lessons dragged. I couldn't get Mum's comments out of my mind. After a great day yesterday, what she'd said was a real downer. I saw Elizabeth briefly at lunch break, and she agreed.

Our mood hadn't changed as we met Mum at the gates.

"Good day at school?" asked Mum.

"Well, no, not really," I said. I had to get it out in the open. "Neither of us could concentrate on our lessons. We kept thinking about the comments you made."

"Oh, dear, that wasn't supposed to happen. I thought you'd understand my concern for all our safety. I didn't mean that we won't be going on any more trips, just that I'm not going to say things just as they come into my head."

"It didn't sound like that, Mum," I said, unconvinced. "And after everyone had such a great time yesterday, we couldn't believe you were shutting Nifty down."

She turned and bent down to us. "Look, children, this is important. Nifty, if used badly, could be dangerous. I won't let that happen. I need you to concentrate on your education. Dad's working, so should you. If you get your chores and all your homework done, then, and only then, we'll see about another experiment with Nifty. But not on school days. Now enough of this, you owe me and your teacher some good homework to make up for today."

"Yes, Mum," I said, and Belle nodded.

We walked home and arrived just as the rain started. I wondered if the weather felt sorry for me and Elizabeth.

We went upstairs to do homework and tried to do as much as we could to catch up on our day.

Mum called us down when Dad arrived.

"Mum's made us a lovely chicken roast today as a bit of a treat. And she wants to talk to us about something important."

We took our seats, and dinner was served.

Mum began to pour the gravy on Dad's plate. "Mr Adams, the funeral director, called and he asked me to go and see him to close Grandad's funeral arrangements. I said that I thought we had, but he said there was one more thing before he could call it complete."

We all looked at her, no one taking a bite of food.

"Let's eat, and you can all try to guess what it was about. I know I spent quite a lot of time thinking about it."

"Can we have some guesses now, or are you going to make us wait until after dinner?" asked Dad.

"I think we should just enjoy the meal and save your thoughts until after. Much more interesting like that."

Was there an evil streak in my mother? I looked at Elizabeth and she shrugged. I had no idea what it could be so just began to eat Mum's amazing meal.

After I'd cleared the plates, Mum told us to go and sit in the lounge.

"Any ideas about the phone call?"

"The only thing I came up with was that there might be a refund or an extra charge to the estate," said Dad.

"I thought that," Mum said, seemingly happy to continue her little game. "But no, it wasn't that."

"I hope it wasn't to ask for Nifty to go to someone else," I said.

"Goodness, no, definitely not that," said Mum, and she turned to Elizabeth.

Elizabeth just shrugged her shoulders. "I don't know."

"Okay," Mum continued. "I met Mr Adams at lunch time. He said, "Please sit down, Mrs Short, while I find the paperwork for you to sign and the box I must give you.""

We all smiled at her trying to sound like Mr Adams.

"I said, 'Box, Mr Adams? Why do I need a box? Are you going to give me a large pile of papers to put in it?' And he replied, 'No, nothing like that.' He then turned to me and said, 'These are your grandad's ashes and as requested, are now in the box that he supplied.' Well, I said that I had no idea that he wanted me to receive his ashes and asked him why he didn't tell me about it before the funeral. He said, 'I had instructions not to.'"

"That's strange," said Dad.

Mum was in full flow and it was hard not to giggle.

"That's what I said. 'What am I supposed to do with them?' I asked him. He gave me this." Mum held out an envelope. "He said that the answer was probably in it and that he was instructed to give it to me when I collected the ashes."

Mum then got up, walked into the kitchen, and came back with a wooden box with lots of carvings on it.

"So here's Grandad," said Mum.

"It's a nice box. Looks Oriental. But what do we do with it?" asked Dad.

"Let me read the letter to you."

Mum opened a hand-written piece of paper and began to read out loud.

Wendy,

If you're reading this, then I'm dead. You've been very good to me over the years, and I showed very little gratitude. Your father was actually my brother, and he married my only true love— your mother. You should've been calling me Uncle, but I didn't want to have anything to do with your father or his family. I hated him and decided I couldn't stay in the country that he and she lived in. It was too painful. While travelling the world, I found out how their lives were going on by slipping

back to see them without them knowing.
I found out that my love had died giving
birth to you.
In all my travels, I never found another
like her, and I never did get married.
You never knew your mother, but she
was a wonderful woman. She seems to
have passed this onto you, because you
never gave up on me, even when I was
intolerable.
I know I looked older than I was. I
had a heart attack in South Africa, and
that took its toll on my life expectancy,
along with the creeping death of cancer
that the doctors said would take me if
I didn't start to look after myself. But
what was the point in that?
I'd returned from time to time with the
help of my little camper van over the
many years and saw you growing up from
afar.
When your father died, I came back,
and that's when we met and I told you
I was your grandfather.
It wasn't hard to lie to you, then. I
must have looked the part, but I wish
now that I'd been honest.
This letter is my request to you to take
my ashes and give them to the monks in

Nepal. They'll be expecting you.
My camper van, now yours, knows where
to go.
Please find it in your heart to forgive me.

As she finished reading the letter, she looked up at us to find us with our mouths open, staring at her.

"Well, it looks as if you had the same reaction as I did. Grandad Rowland was my uncle, not my grandad. How stupid is all of this? I didn't even know that I had an uncle. Dad never said anything about him, and he never sent a birthday or Christmas card to any of us."

"Hardly surprising considering what he said in the letter," Dad said. "He was hurting with lost love. It must've been hard for him to look at either of them. That's why he went abroad, to try to forget."

"But he said he kept coming back to check up on them and me, after I was born."

"I guess he didn't want to completely give up on his brother and the love of his life. Your mother must have been quite a lady. He must have had great difficulty trying not to blame you for your Mother's death."

"Yes, George, you're probably right."

"So, what's going to happen now, Mum?" I asked. "Are you going to Nepal to give your uncle's ashes to the monks?"

"Firstly, I'm going to carry on calling him Grandad. Secondly, it was a request to take his ashes, and I don't feel inclined to do that at the moment. And lastly, if I am going to go to Nepal, then we're all going."

"Wow-wee, Mum," I exclaimed. "I like the last bit. Isn't Nepal where Mount Everest is?"

"It is, Daniel. Well done!" said Dad.

"When can we go?" I asked.

"*If* I decide to go, it won't be until school term ends. Then if we want to stay for a day or two, we can. But, if you want to convince me to take you, I want total concentration on your school work for the rest of the two weeks and good reports."

I nodded and saw Elizabeth doing the same. Nepal was thousands of miles away, but I knew that Mum could easily go on her own and be back in half an hour! I didn't want to miss out on a trip like that!

Chapter Fourteen
Two Weeks Passing

I woke the next morning with my mind buzzing with all sorts of thoughts. Grandad was actually my mum's uncle, making him my great uncle, not my grandad! And even more exciting, how two brothers had fallen in love with the same woman and then never spoken again! It was like a movie, and Elizabeth said she thought it was very romantic.

We got ready for school, and once ready, set out to walk to school, just as it started to rain. I'd been praying for the weather to take a turn for the worse in the hope it might mean Mum would employ Nifty. I was getting used to being a time traveller.

"I'll lock up. You get into Nifty. No point in getting very wet."

Elizabeth and I went out and Mum joined us shortly after.

"We're taking the children to school, Nifty."

Mum did her usual thing after we were all safely inside and we appeared by the side road.

It was still raining, so Mum put up the umbrella and took us all the way to the school door before saying good-bye.

"Work hard, little sis. This is for Mount Everest!"

I said to encourage Belle. I wanted this trip more than anything.

***

School went painfully slow over the next two weeks. The only excitement was the auctioneer (gargoyle guy) calling to say that all of the lots had gone in the general auction, and the special items that had been passed to another auction house had also been sold. Mum asked him how much the total was after he'd had his cut, as she called it. I don't know how much he said, but she had to sit down from the shock.

A cheque arrived two days later, and it had the same effect on her. Dad told us that we'd never had so much money in one go, and it was something that Mum and the rest of us would need to adjust to.

The weekend came, and Mum and Dad met with someone from a local charity and they took Grandad's furniture away. That cleared the house for the makeover they wanted for the house to sell. They had quotes from a few decorators before settling on a father and son who were highly recommended by one of our neighbours. Mum gave them the keys, and they said they'd start on Monday.

We started our final week at school, and on Tuesday Mr Plumber rang. He wanted to visit the house to see if Grandad's camper van was in our garage. Mum agreed to meet him on Thursday.

He looked at the van and nodded. "I'm satisfied that you're upholding Mr Rowland's request, but I'll have to return in a year to see that you still have the van."

On Friday, our last day at end of term, we had a party and said good-bye to friends. My best friend,

Garry, was going to the Greek islands. His parents had booked a boat that would take them all around them. Garry said they'd be working on board and help with the sailing of it, as well as eating and sleeping on it. It sounded wonderful.

Garry asked if we were going anywhere, and I hesitated before answering. How could I say we might be going to Nepal in a magic camper van?

Instead, I opted for, "I don't know what plans my parents have. We usually sort something out once we're in school holidays. We might have a week away somewhere in England in a caravan or a tent," I said.

Garry smiled at that. He knew we didn't go abroad.

I hated lying, to him, but it seemed less crazy than telling the truth.

"See you later this evening," Garry said and linked up with his mother.

We left school and went our own way. Elizabeth and I were walking home together as part of our "joint responsibility of taking care of each other." I didn't mind. I'm happy to look after my little sis; it's all part of being a big brother.

We talked a little about our new adventure. Well, we hoped there was going to be an adventure because nothing had been mentioned for a whole week. As we walked home, we talked about what Nepal might be like. Would it be warmer there or very cold? It was a typical summer's day for the UK.

We got home, sorted our bags out, passed our end of term reports to Mum, and then went upstairs to change.

Elizabeth and I returned downstairs and saw that Mum was reading our reports. We stayed quiet until she'd finished. She placed her reading glasses down and looked at us.

"Well, having read these reports...I think this family will be going to Nepal."

Elizabeth and I jumped up and down, and I pulled her into a big hug.

"Don't forget that this is about honouring Grandad's request—it's not just a holiday. Your Dad and I were hoping for good results, so we've been discussing the arrangements for a week's holiday. We don't know how long we'll be in Nepal, but we'll stay a few days. It's a foreign country, and we don't know what to expect."

I hugged Mum, and Elizabeth joined in.

"Elizabeth, you have your singing practice tonight, so let's get dinner sorted. Daniel, it's your judo practice, isn't it? Garry's mother rang to say she'd pick you up if it's raining, but Garry will call for you as usual if it's dry. If it's raining when you finish, wait under cover and Dad or I will collect both of you. Elizabeth, you'll be collected as usual."

Dad came home and went up to change. He returned a little later to sit and wait while Mum finished the dinner.

Once they were done, Mum called us to the table, and we ate well.

Mum told Dad about our reports and he read them for himself.

"That's really great, kids. Well done for working so hard this year," said Dad.

Elizabeth and I smiled, but what we really wanted to talk about was Nepal.

Dad placed his knife and fork down on his empty plate. "Your mother and I have been talking about the request to deliver her uncle's—"

"Grandad's," Mum said and gave him one of her

special looks.

"Sorry, Wendy. About Grandad's request for his ashes."

Mum nodded.

"We've talked about the instructions and how Nifty knows the way to get there. But we've got no knowledge of the country, visa requirements, injections, or food. How do we cope? We're really out of our comfort zone on this."

I smiled, mostly at their worry about food. How different could it be? "But, Dad, lots of people go to these places...and they manage okay, don't they?"

"You're partly right, Daniel, but we won't be going into the country through normal channels. Because of Nifty, we'll bypass all the usual security and just appear in the country."

"We want to do this, but we've going to be very careful with officials and be prepared to order Nifty to return us home very quickly if there's any trouble," said Mum.

"So with all things, there's got to be some rules," Dad continued, "and they're very important. Firstly, you're not to wander away from us. If we call you, you come to us immediately. Don't make us ask twice." We nodded. "Secondly, don't point at things because in many countries that's considered an insult. Motioning at something with an open hand is more friendly. Lastly, we don't know where Nifty is taking us in Nepal. We assume we'll just appear at the place we need to pass Grandad's ashes to, but we don't know. So we have to be prepared for anything!"

"Food is another thing," said Mum. "Lots of people in foreign countries eat bugs, snakes, lizards, just about anything. I saw it on one of the travel shows on TV. I have no intention of joining them if they do. I'll be cooking lots of chicken, and I'll take pasta, rice, and noodles—all things that I can cook up quickly. I've never been abroad, so I have no idea what to expect."

"Any questions?" asked Dad.

"Actually, yes. Are we just going to this place to deliver Grandad's ashes or will we also be going to other places?"

"We want to do that, Daniel, but we'll need to see how we get on with our delivering Grandad's ashes first."

With our discussion ended, we cleared the meal debris and got ready for our clubs.

We had a lot to look forward to, and I couldn't wait to get started.

Chapter Fifteen
Getting There

As the week passed, Mum was true to her word and cooked lots of chicken legs, thighs, and breasts. It seemed like a waste of time to me; I wanted to try the food Nepal had to offer—even if it was insects! Dad came home after his last day at work and said, "That's it, I'm done for the week. Holiday time, kids!"

Elizabeth and I made sure our cameras and iPads were charged, and Mum packed us enough clothes for a month! She'd got pills for upset stomachs, toilet rolls, air fresheners, almost our entire house was there for Dad to pack. He loaded everything into Nifty ready to start our big adventure the next morning.

I didn't sleep well. I couldn't settle my racing mind, full of thoughts of the excitement to come; Nepal, Mount Everest, monks! I was about to see all of those things AND it was my first time out of England. All our other holidays had been in caravans. Now we had a camper van that could slip through time to wherever Mum told it go! I couldn't believe our luck.

I woke feeling very tired but rushed to get dressed and went downstairs. Mum was busy laying cups out as I sank onto one of the breakfast chairs.

"Good morning, Daniel," she said. "I hope you

slept well and are feeling bright-eyed and bushy-tailed ready for the start of our big day? You don't look like you are."

I didn't reply. I just rested my head in my hands and closed my eyes.

"Bed is the place to sleep, young man. Wake yourself up and make yourself useful."

"Oh, Mum, just leave me to thaw out. I didn't get much sleep last night. I kept going over the whole day, what could happen, and what we might see. I just couldn't stop my mind racing with ideas of sights and sounds."

"And now you're going to miss it all as you sleep in Nifty for the day. Daniel, you really are a case!"

I thought about that for a minute or two. She was right, and I didn't want to miss a second of this. Time to buck up. "Do you want me to take anything out and put it in Nifty?"

"Not yet. If you could get the tea ready, that'd be a great help."

I did as asked, arranged the mugs in a tidy line like little soldiers, put the tea bags in, and put teaspoons near each one. Mum poured the hot water, and I stirred the tea to get the best flavour from them. I liked mine nice and weak, and I pulled the teabag out almost straight away. Dad liked it super strong, but his always tasted very bitter to me.

Dad came in and snaffled his mug. "Well done, Daniel, you made mine just in time."

I took the teabags from the other two mugs, then added milk. Not wanting any milk in mine, I picked up my cup and followed Dad into the lounge. Elizabeth came downstairs, mumbled hello, and went into the kitchen. Mum called us to get our breakfast.

We all munched our breakfast quickly, and it was

clear everyone was eager to get going. Mum put some food bags onto the work surface. "I'm going out to Nifty. Will you bring things as I call for them? Frozen things are in the bottom drawer of the freezer."

Once Nifty was open, she stepped in, told it to give room for us to move around, and then waited for the shaking to stop.

She opened the long cupboard and said, "I'll need a fridge freezer in here, Nifty. Can you arrange that?"

Nifty shook, expanded, and gave Mum the fridge freezer she'd asked for.

She opened the door. "It'll need to be very cold, Nifty. Can you turn it on, please?"

Another shake, and she opened the freezer section once more. Nifty had not only turned it on, it'd made it icy cold instantly. Nifty was full of surprises!

"Right, Daniel, time to load the frozen chicken. Would you organise a relay between you, Dad, and Elizabeth, and I'll load the freezer."

I went back to the kitchen, told them Mum's wishes, and took the first bag of chicken to Mum with Elizabeth following just after.

Once that was in, we loaded milk, yoghurts, and other food bits. One thing for sure, we weren't going to starve!

Mum closed the fridge freezer's doors and moved to the rear of Nifty and looked at the toilet. "It'd be good to have a bathroom with a shower and a toilet, Nifty," she said.

Nifty gave a shake and the bathroom's appearance changed to a shower cubicle with a toilet next to it. Mum placed toilet rolls in it and soap to wash our hands. Finally, she was finished, and Elizabeth went into the house to tell Dad to lock up and then join us.

Dad came out and climbed into Nifty. "If we find

we've left anything, we can always come back," said Mum.

Dad looked at her and grinned. "Wendy, if you've forgotten anything, I'll be very surprised!"

She raised her eyebrow. "Did you pick up Grandad's ashes?"

"Oh no! The box is still on the mantelpiece."

"George, they're the very reason we're doing this!"

"Okay, Wendy. I'll get it."

We waited for Dad to return, and he climbed back into Nifty with the box.

"Grandad's with us safe and sound now. Sorry, Wendy. Not like me to forget."

Mum said nothing but gave him one of her funny looks as he shut the driver's door and sat behind the driving wheel.

"Well, if everyone's ready, I think we should get on our way. Nifty, we need to deliver Grandad's ashes to their final resting place, and I understand you know where. Would you take us there, please?"

Nifty gave a shake, and we were there…well, we were somewhere.

We seemed to be parked in a lay-by, and we were looking down a stone road track on the side of a mountain road where lorries were crossing a stream and making their way up to us.

The first lorry passed us, followed by a bus filled with local people. Next a flatbed truck with a load on it that looked to be far too much for it. People were sat on top of it.

Eight or nine vehicles passed us, and as the last one came up the hill and passed us, Nifty pulled out and drove down over the hill, then across the river, and started up the hill on the other side.

"Nifty, can't you just take us to the place we need

to go? It surely isn't necessary for you to drive along the roads like this?"

Nifty kept going ever upward.

"George, open the door. That will stop it. We're going higher and higher up the side of this mountain, and I really don't like it at all."

"Wendy, I can't open the door," said Dad. "I'm not driving, Nifty is doing everything. Try to not look down and trust Nifty."

Mum looked a very strange colour!

Nifty reached a sharp bend on the way still climbing, and as it started to go around the corner, we met a lorry.

The lorry driver braked, and Nifty stopped.

A great rock overhang was in front of us with enough room for one and a half vehicles.

Nifty reversed back to the corner, and the lorry came on.

It pulled in close to the rock, the top of the lorry just missing the overhang, then Nifty pulled forward, almost touching the lorry. It slowly drove past the lorry.

I was looking out of the back window, and it seemed that only two wheels on Nifty could be on the road. My view was straight down!

This can't be happening—only two wheels on the track. I didn't say anything to Mum in case it made her panic even more. Elizabeth looked at me as if to ask if everything was okay and I smiled. *Fingers and toes crossed.*

Nifty pulled back onto the track and continued on its way. We went up the carved track, and as we rounded another corner, found a wider ledge had been cut to allow two vehicles to pass.

Nifty pulled in to the side as another convoy of lorries, buses, and a few motorbikes crossed a wooden bridge from their side to us and passed us.

"I just need to go to the toilet," called Mum as she rushed towards the bathroom.

Vehicles just kept coming and Nifty waited.

I was excited, and maybe a little scared, but I couldn't take my eyes from all that was going on.

One lorry came past us and had people hanging onto the sides of it.

Finally Nifty was able to pull out and with a clear road in front of us and across the bridge. We drove down a slight slope then started to cross the bridge.

Mum came back as Nifty was halfway over the bridge. She looked to the left at the sheer drop then to the right. This view was a sheer drop, but there were mountains in the distance.

"I might need the toilet again. Don't worry about

me. I'll be back."

I got up and made Mum a drink of elderflower water.

When she returned, I said, "Why don't you lay down on the settee, have a drink of this, and try not to worry. Nifty seems to have everything in control, so try to relax."

"Thank you, I think I will do that, Daniel."

She lay down as Nifty finished the bridge crossing and started climbing once again on a track cut into the side of the mountain.

This side had enough room for two vehicles but large concrete blocks had been put at the side nearest to the drop, and they prevented two vehicles from being side by side.

Lots of loose stones were on the track but just like the other side, it was pretty rough track with deep ruts from the lorries and other traffic that had passed along their way.

Nifty continued on upwards, and even more vehicles came down.

It was getting colder, and I could see the snow on the peaks of the mountains across the ravine that we were still climbing up.

Just as it seemed everyone might be getting restless about how much further, Nifty turned a corner, and drove down a slope with a hairpin corner at the bottom. Nifty started to speed up.

"We seem to be out of control," Dad whispered to me over his shoulder. "We're never going to make it around that corner at this speed." He looked further behind to Mum. "Hang on to anything you can," Dad called out.

I dashed over to Mum and put my hands around her with Elizabeth taking Mum's legs.

"Whatever is going on?" Mum shouted.
"No, Nifty!" Dad exclaimed.
I shut my eyes, took a big breath, and waited for the crash.

Chapter Sixteen
Ashes to Monks

It never came. The inside of Nifty went completely black as if we were going through a tunnel. As that thought came to me, so the light at the end of the tunnel also came. Nifty drove out of it and onto a track that again was on the side of a mountain range.

As we all stood to look out of the window, Mum's question came again as she stood having been pinned by her children to her prone position.

"Whatever is going on?"

"I thought we were going to crash, Wendy," said Dad. "We were hurtling down a slope with a very tight U-bend at the bottom, and I didn't think we'd make it. I thought we were going to crash!"

"But we must've got around the corner somehow, because I can see a valley below. Look at the colour and those buildings," I said, instantly mesmerised.

"We didn't make it, Wendy. We just hit the rocks at the bottom where the U-bend was, and Nifty just drove straight through them!"

I looked back up the track we were on and was amazed to see the tunnel mouth fade to nothing. The road now ended against the cliff face!

As we descended, I marvelled at the beauty.

A mixture of different types of green trees were everywhere. Some seemed to have fruit, others had masses of coloured flowers. I could see a river flowing through the valley and temple like structures in a clearing.

Nifty followed the track down the side of the mountain, and we were soon going under the trees, following the smooth and flat track.

Birds flew over us, and we shouted out to each other and pointed.

Mum moved forward and sat next to Dad. "This is beautiful, George. I didn't know what to expect, but this is wonderful."

"Are you feeling okay now, Wendy?" Dad asked.

"Yes, George, I am. It's as if that didn't happen. I think the wonderful views have helped to relax me."

"Elephants," I shouted to Elizabeth and pointed to the front.

Everyone looked as a herd of elephants walked from under the trees and started to cross the track.

Nifty slowed and stopped as they made their way across, the biggest first, then a mixture of little and big ones.

Once they'd gone into the trees, Nifty started to move again.

Butterflies of all sorts of colours passed by, visiting the flowers along the track's edge and diving in under the trees.

Eventually, Nifty slowed down, and we came out into the open area we had seen with buildings in it.

And what magnificent buildings they were!

Set in the centre of the clearing was a huge temple. It was circular with steps going up to another level that was flat and people in coloured clothes could be seen walking around.

The open doors to the temple were directly in front of the steps, and the temple rose up like cake tiers with a point on the top.

The colours of the temple were shades of red, orange, and yellow. Coloured triangle flags were fixed at each level, and followed the steps down to end on poles, standing on the outside of the temple.

Other buildings surrounded the temple, built to face the temple thus giving a circular roadway around the vast temple. People were coming and going from these. It seemed a very busy place.

I was so fascinated by everything I was seeing that I failed to notice that Nifty had stopped.

Nifty opened the door on Dad's side. He looked at Mum. "It would seem that we're supposed to get out now."

They both got out of the van, and we quickly followed.

Men were walking around in long flowing tops with baggy trousers underneath. They had what looked like a T-shirt on under their flowing coat. This was tucked into the baggy trousers. They wore no shoes but had bracelets on their ankles. They were all bald! Not a bit of hair could be seen. These must be the monks Grandad mentioned in his letter!

They wore one single colour. If they had a yellow top then the T-shirt and baggy trousers were also the same colour.

The ranges of colour varied from the yellow we had observed. Some wore a set in light brown and another wore an orange set. In all cases, they had matching trousers and T-shirt.

As we stood together looking around, a man came down the steps from the temple and looked as if he was coming towards us.

He was in similar clothing but this was a red colour. His ankle bracelet was also in red. He stepped down from the last step, put his hands together, and bowed to us. Dad put his hands together and did the same, and the rest of us followed his example.

The man smiled, and he came up to us. "Welcome. You have been expected."

Mum and Dad looked at each other, then Dad turned to the man. "How could you expect us? We only decided to come here—wherever here is—yesterday."

"We were told by your ancestor, now departed, that you were on your way. This is why we prepared your pathway to bring you here and to bring our brother home. You travelled in his footsteps, along the outside roadway just as he did to come here."

"Maybe I'm a little slow on my understanding on this," said Mum, "but are you saying that the ashes of our Grandad Rowland told you we were coming here?"

The red monk nodded. "You understand correctly."

"I don't understand. What are you telling us?" Dad asked.

"You burned the outer shell of your ancestor, but his 'self' lives on. You may know this as a soul, a spirit, whatever word you wish to use to describe the self of the man. It is this that conveyed to us that you intended to come to us."

Mum looked puzzled as Dad was. "You're suggesting that we've got our Grandad's ashes, but that his spirit, his inner being, is somewhere else?"

"You are correct," said the red monk.

"Grandad's spirit that told you we were coming to bring his ashes—exactly *where* is he?"

Red monk stepped aside and lifted his arm. He motioned his open palm toward our camper van.

"Grandad Rowland is inside the camper van?"

Mum asked, clearly not convinced.

"His inner self is now within the vehicle you came in. He told us he was on his way, and we made our arrangements for you to enter this holy place."

"Speaking of this place," said Dad. "Where exactly are we?"

"You may know of it as Utopia or Shangri-La. People call this place by many names but few find their way to it. It is written that we exist between the Kunlun Mountains, but we know nothing of this. We exist to meditate and seek enlightenment within our minds and our inner self."

We were still looking at Nifty as the red monk spoke. I had so many questions, but I guessed Mum and Dad would ask them all for me!

"Are you saying that the camper van *is* our Grandad?" asked Mum.

"No, Mistress, but the power that brings you among us is his power within the vehicle. His inner self, his spark of life, this is the motivation that brings your vehicle to this place."

Mum seemed to be getting more and more flustered but the red monk stayed strangely calm.

"Can I ask a question, please?" I said putting my hand up as if in school.

"Most certainly, young person. What do you wish to know?"

"If Nifty, I mean Grandad, knew that he was coming here, why didn't he just appear here instead of coming along those frightening cliff roads?"

"Ah, yes, it is our way. Our brother did a small pilgrimage by coming on the road, as did you all."

"But why?" said Mum. "Why would he wish us to bring his ashes here? What are you going to do with them?"

The red monk smiled gently. "Our Lama will grant you an audience, and he will explain why your ancestor is important to us."

I turned to Elizabeth. "They have Llamas that talk. This is an amazing place. I wonder if the elephants talk too. Maybe this place is magic like our camper van!"

Dad laughed. "The Lama is the highest position in monk orders. It's not an animal, so none will be talking to you, but I like your thinking, Daniel."

"Oh," I muttered, disappointed that the magic stopped with our camper van.

"We do not usually allow women into our domain, but our Lama has granted you an audience."

"Why no women?" asked Mum in her harsh voice. *Watch out, red monk!*

"Our order is male only. There is an order that is all women, and they, like us, seek the higher plains of thought. There are no distractions with thoughts of procreation. We can devote our time to other thoughts. This is so with the women's order. No men would be allowed into their domain." He turned and started up the steps. "If you will follow me, my master, the Lama, will receive you now. Can you bring our brothers ashes with you? He will then receive them into his care."

Dad turned and looked at me. "Would you go and fetch the box please, Daniel?"

As the rest of my family followed the red monk up the steps, I went to Nifty. I opened the door and reached into the glove compartment that Dad had put the box in.

"Very reverent, Dad," I said as I pulled Grandad out from himself!

I held Grandad tightly under my arm and climbed up the steps. I joined the others just as the red monk stopped and turned to our group.

"I will take you to single rooms, and you will be asked to change into the white robes provided. Please take your shoes from your feet before entering our temple. You may take them with you."

The temple was all wooden built. Large pillars held the roof above us and between the pillars were planks fitted as slats with a gap to allow air to pass through. It was decorated with bright colours and some paintings.

We were shown into the first area, and the red monk pointed to four small cubicles.

"Please place all of your other world's clothing in the box provided and put on the clothes you will find in each room," he said. "Once you are prepared, please join me out here."

We each went into the cubicles. A box with white robes was on a bench.

I pulled the baggy trousers out and measured them against me. They looked like they'd fit me. I put my socks and shoes in the box. I took my tracksuit bottoms off and pulled my new baggy trousers on. I pulled off my shirt and replaced it with their T-shirt. Lastly, I pulled the long white coat over my shoulders and slipped my arms into the sleeves.

I was ready! Then I saw the one item I hadn't noticed.

White baggy underpants. Yuk!

What was the point of all this? But I changed anyway.

I opened the door and stepped back out to see Dad. He looked quite good in his white gear. "Did you put the white pants on, Dad?"

"I did, Daniel. We're supposed to take *all* of our other world clothes off."

A little later, Mum came out and said in a hushed voice, "They left a pair of pants just like baggy boxers for me. I really don't want to put them on."

"Us too," said Dad. "We've put them on but they're quite itchy. I think we're supposed to divest ourselves of all of the outside worldly things."

"But, George, there's no bra!"

Dad smiled. "Just this once, be brave and proud, Wendy. Take your watch off, put those lovely pants on, and pull the coat around you. Then the other monks will not have lascivious thoughts about you."

Mum looked at Dad, gave a little smirk, and returned to her cubicle.

Elizabeth came out with a look of disgust as she held the white pants out in front of her.

Dad laughed. "I know, darling. Just pop them on. I'm sure this won't take long."

Mum came out, whispered to Elizabeth, and she went back into her cubicle.

When we were all ready, we stood looking at the inside of the building.

"I will be your escort to the inner chamber. Will you come this way?"

We turned to see the person who had spoken to us and saw a man like our red monk, but this one was dressed in an orange coloured set of clothes.

"You have divested yourselves of all of the outside world's things and are now ready to see the Master. You have kept rings on your fingers, but this is a sign of love, and we would not wish to break this bond. Will you bring the casket holding our brother and follow me?"

Dad turned to me, and I held it up. He smiled and then we followed the monk. We came to the inner area and saw mats laid on the floor. Upon a plinth a monk in very deep purple sat on a stone looking down on us.

"May I have the casket?" asked the orange monk who had led us in. I passed it to him. "Please sit," he said and pointed to the mats.

We sat down on the woven mats and waited as the monk took the casket up to the purple monk.

Once it was in the hands of the purple monk, the orange monk withdrew.

Purple monk, who we took to be the Lama, placed the casket on a small table.

"I understand that you wish to know why we would receive our brother here."

Dad nodded slowly. *I definitely would.*

"Your relative was a very troubled and bitter man when he arrived here. He was in the city of Kathmandu and was living in the vehicle you arrived in. One of our novices in yellow was working amongst the people there. Two undesirables berated his calling and then beat him. He was pushed to the floor. The undesirables then started to kick our novice."

He shuddered as if he could see the attack in his mind.

"Your relative came upon the scene and rushed to his aid. He pulled one away then returned for the second. He used a minimum of force and drew the second away. He then stood over our novice who had been kicked in the head many times and was not moving. The undesirables attacked him, and one struck him with a knife."

Mum gasped, and I had visions of Grandad stood over the monk on the floor with his walking stick ready! But of course, he would have been different then to how I was remembering him.

The monk went on after a brief pause. "Still he stood over our novice, and he received yet another knife wound. As he fell over the body of our novice, the authorities arrived and the undesirables were taken away. A message came to us, and we claimed both as our brotherhood's people. They were conveyed to us, and we tended their wounds."

Mum made a slight noise, and I saw her wipe her eye with the end of her coat.

"Unfortunately our novice had left this place, and we blessed his departure," the monk said as he looked down at us. He paused and looked at the casket. "Your relative slowly recovered and his wounds healed, save for the one troubling his mind. He was offered the chance to talk to our brothers, and he took the yellow robes of our departed novice."

Grandad was a monk! He had long shaggy hair, but these guys are all bald.

"He spoke of his love for the one who had spurned his advances. He spoke of his shame for turning his back on his brother, who had received the love of the one he would wish to have."

He paused, and once again Mum wiped her eyes.

I glanced at Belle and saw she had a few tears falling down her cheek.

"As time advanced with us, so your relative renounced his hate. One day, he asked to leave and to return to see his brother in your world to ask his forgiveness."

So that was when Grandad came back to see his brother and his wife.

"I spoke to him, and we agreed that when he departed his world, his body should be returned to us. He asked a boon of us, this being, once his existence on your world ended, he would like his 'spark of life,' his inner being, his soul, whatever you would call it, to be placed as a guardian to watch over his brother or over his brother's love."

The story was beginning to get to every one of us as we sat and listened. I was trying to not shed a tear, but Elizabeth and Mum were now openly sobbing.

"It was spoken about over many meetings with me and then the answer came to us. When the time came, he was to direct his soul to the vehicle in which he had come. As part of this device, he could watch over and protect those he would once again share his heart with."

He turned, looked at the casket once again, and placed his hand on it and rubbed it for a few moments, almost lovingly.

Again he turned to us and continued, "Our brother left us shortly after and we never saw him again until we had notice of his request to return. The rest you know. It would appear that his demons within him rose again, and he fought them to the end."

The Lama looked at the casket and then continued. "He was a good man, and it would be our wish that you welcome your relative into your heart for you will travel many places in your world before we receive his soul to reunite him to his resting place. This is his home, and when he wants to return, so it shall be."

The Lama stood and walked from the plinth into a room at the side carrying the casket with the ashes.

The orange monk returned and led us from the inner area back to our cubicles.

"Please divest yourselves of the robes and dress in the clothes of the outside world you came in. I will wait for you here."

We went to our cubicles and changed back into our original clothing. Lots of new information raced around my mind, not least, that Nifty was Grandad and he was a hero and a monk!

It seemed quite far-fetched but then again, any vehicle that could magic itself around the world wasn't "normal," so what was?

Once we were dressed, we exited the cubicles and

again followed the orange monk outside.

We looked down at Nifty, still where we'd left him cooking in the hot sun.

The red monk took over and escorted us down the steps.

He turned to us as we came up to Nifty. "If you will return to your vehicle, it will return you to your own world. Peace be with you and to your relative, our brother."

He turned to Mum. "Find in your heart forgiveness and share the blessing bestowed upon your family. Take each day as it is given to you and use it wisely, for you will never know when it may be your last. True Nirvana, Utopia, or Shangri-La is all around you. Be at peace with your world and these mythical places will become part of your heart."

Mum was the last to get into Nifty. She took one last look at the red monk then shut the door.

Nifty started to move forward and drove in a circle around the temple.

Lots of monks stood on the steps waving as we made the circle and then started up the track. Slowly we climbed upward and came towards the solid wall, then Nifty slowed.

Mum moved forward and sat in the front seat, and then Nifty started moving forward again for as we had slowed, so the tunnel had reappeared.

The end of the track came and Nifty just drove straight into the tunnel. It seemed a short tunnel but just before we emerged on the other side, Nifty paused. The exit before us was opaque, and we could see lorries passing and buses. I guess that they couldn't see us because when there were no vehicles, Nifty pulled out and started to drive along the track from the U-bend still moving along the way we had been going.

We were all very quiet. I was thinking about what had happened and what Grandad had gone through. I was happy to be on holiday in a new and exciting place, but sadness tugged at my heart as I thought about Grandad keeping all of this to himself all this time.

Chapter Seventeen
Tiger Lodge

We travelled along the track still tight against the mountain but strangely, Mum seemed quite relaxed about it all. I watched her as she stared out over the drop that had terrified her a short while ago. She said nothing but just looked at the view as we went on our way. I wondered if the monks had somehow passed some of their calmness onto Mum.

We had been travelling along the mountainous track for quite a while when we rounded a bend and saw that the track split; one continued on around the mountain, the other started to drop down the side of mountain. Nifty took the track going down.

We'd met a few lorries and buses climbing up as we descended and passed them without a word from Mum. Dad must've got a little worried as was I.

He turned to Mum. "Are you okay, Wendy?"

She looked at Dad. "Well, no, George. I'm feeling quite ashamed of myself. I've been going over everything the lama told us; the story of my uncle's bravery and the death of that poor boy." Mum shifted in her seat, so she was talking to all of us. "Then the counselling with the monks, trying to come to terms with the fact that his love for my mother could never come to fruition. George, it's so romantic I could cry. His love for her was so strong that it burned his love for his brother and changed it to hatred."

She paused, took a deep breath, and went on to say, "What a pity he didn't tell me. He must've gone through a lot of torment. I'm glad we delivered his ashes and heard his story. I think it's given me a sort of peace with our relationship."

Nifty must've been listening, because he gave a toot on his horn.

"So, Wendy, are you going to call Nifty, Uncle, from now on?" Dad asked.

"I only knew my uncle as Grandad, and he'll always be that to me. That won't lessen my love or respect for him. That's been enhanced by our new knowledge about him. I can't change the past, but he's my Nifty now, and he's watching over us all. Let's just share whatever journeys we take together in the knowledge that we're a family united by a magical camper van."

No one said anything for quite a while. I couldn't think of anything appropriate to say.

Then I noticed that we'd descended into the valley. "Look, everyone, we're on the valley floor, and it's widening out."

Tall grass higher than a house came almost up to the roadway we were following. It was still a dirt road but was quite even. Trees seemed to be in competition to grow upward, but it looked as if the grass was winning.

We came to a junction and started to rise on the track's route.

We climbed a small hill to bring us up above the top of the grass, and as we levelled, the vista before us was something else.

"Oh, George, what a splendid view. I need to take

a photo of that. It's just so beautiful."

Nifty stopped and the front doors opened, and everyone got out.

It was truly a wonderful sight.

In front of us was a mass of tall grass heads swaying in the breeze, the colours changing from gold to yellow, to almost silver as the breeze played with the heads. We could see across the valley to a river beyond the tall grass. The other side of the river had brown mud banks and was slightly higher than our side, which had bushes, trees, and small clumps of the tall grass nearer to the water's edge.

Dad turned to us. "I think that's called elephant grass. I saw it on a wildlife programme once."

We took our photos, got back into Nifty, and went on our way once again.

"I'm going to get a cold drink for everyone, Nifty, so please try to avoid big bumps."

I'm not sure what happened, but it felt that Nifty raised a little bit. We followed the track through the trees super smoothly and into a jungle.

Mum handed out drinks. "Thank you, Nifty."

And again I felt we dropped a few inches because we started to rock a little as Nifty drove on.

We climbed a little more and then came out into an open plain with flowers growing on and below the trees. There were large wooden house-like buildings on stilts.

Nifty drove up to one, turned, and stopped below it.

The front doors opened, so Mum and Dad got out, followed by Elizabeth and me.

A man came down the stairs and put his hands together as if in prayer and bowed to us. "Welcome to Tiger Lodge. My name is Batsa. You must be the Short family?"

"We are. And you have a booking for us?" asked Dad, who returned the bow. He then looked around at all of us, and we did the same.

"Oh yes, Sir. Your secretary paid for a two-night stay. We just need you to sign the register. We have been faxed a copy of your passports and your short-term entry visa. If you will follow me, I will take you to your house."

Mum looked at Dad who raised his hands and looked just as amazed as I was feeling. Nifty had organised our stay.

It was lovely and cool inside the reception area, and a lady came over to us with a tray of drinks.

"Please try one of our fruit drinks. It is passion fruit juice."

We all took one then sat in the comfy chairs and waited.

Batsa asked Dad to fill in our address on the form and sign it.

Once this was done and we'd finished our drinks, which I have to say was very nice, we were taken to our house.

We walked over from one building to the other on an open pathway above the grass and scrub below that was like a bridge. We walked past another building then repeated the same access to the next building.

Batsa unlocked the door of this one and showed us around. He pointed out the lounge, the drinks cabinet, and a TV that he said worked now and then as reception was not very good because of the mountains.

"Water bottles will be placed in the fridge for you to make drinks. Should you run out, please ring reception, and we will deliver more. Please don't drink the tap water—it could upset you," said Batsa.

Next, we went into the bedrooms. One was quite large; Mum and Dad claimed it. The other two were small with a single bed and a tall cupboard to put our clothes in.

We were then shown the bathroom and told how to work the shower. You had to pull on a chain hanging in the bathroom, wait for a moment, and then the water would come.

"It is just one temperature," said Batsa. "It comes from the big tank outside and is heated by the sun. Water is at a premium in the jungle, so we save all the shower water and use it on the garden plants."

"Just the shower water?" I asked. "Not the toilet water too?"

"No, young Sir." He smiled. "But maybe we should think about this also." He turned to Mum and Dad. "I'll get the boys to bring your suitcases up to you," said Batsa.

"Do you think we could wait for a short while? I'd like a rest after such a long journey," said Mum.

"Of course, I will leave you then until you are ready. Just return to our reception and we will arrange everything."

He left and closed the door.

Elizabeth and I went to the double doors at the one end of the house and found there was a veranda with chairs outside. The seats looked out over the grass front that dipped down towards the tall elephant grass that we'd seen as we arrived.

"Can we go outside and sit down, please," I asked. "I'd like to look out over the valley."

"Absolutely, Daniel," said Dad.

We all went outside and above us were two windmill fans that Dad switched on. We sat in the chairs and enjoyed the nice cooling breeze.

Dad went back into the house and came out a short while later with a jug of fruit juice and four glasses.

"We need to keep drinking so we can don't dehydrate. It's much hotter than we're used to."

Dad poured the drinks and we sipped it as we sat there, looking over a scene that we would never have believed we'd ever be lucky enough to see.

I snuggled into the cushions in my chair. I was like a king, surveying all I owned.

We saw a troop of monkeys cross over the open area before they disappeared into the trees on the other side.

Then we heard a noise and I looked at Mum. She'd dropped off to sleep!

"Come on, let's get our suitcases sorted. It won't take long, and then we can really settle down and relax," whispered Dad.

We left Mum, returned to Nifty, and grabbed what we needed. The food we had packed stayed in the freezer—I wanted to try all the wonderful things this place could offer us.

Once we got everything, Dad began to lead the way back to the house.

***

When Mum woke up, we went for a walk around the grounds. The flowers were lovely and butterflies were in abundance as we marvelled at all the different kinds. When we returned, there was a message pinned to our door that said evening dinner would be served from seven in the dining room.

"Oh, George, we've got all that chicken in the freezer in Nifty, and I'm not sure I'll like foreign food!" Mum said.

"Well, Wendy, the chicken isn't going anywhere. I think we should make the effort and try something new," Dad responded.

"You like Chinese, Mum. This might not be so different. Let's give it a try," I said.

"Very well. I'll give it a go."

We got changed. Mum insisted that we dress in clean clothes, then just before seven, we headed to the dining area.

Batsa greeted us and escorted us to a table but it was like nothing I'd ever seen before.

It was very low to the floor and they were cushions in front of it.

"What's this, then?" asked Dad.

"In Nepal, we kneel in front of the table to eat," said Batsa.

We all looked at Batsa then at each other. My eyes dropped to the cushions. I looked around at other people and I couldn't see their feet! Was this more magic?!

Batsa must've read my mind because he lifted a cushion and showed us a gap under the table where our legs would hang.

Once we'd settled, Batsa brought us some fruit juices, then a lady dressed in a long gown carried out a plate of fish with steam rising from it.

She knelt by Dad first. "Would you like to try one or both?" she asked.

Dad's eyes widened. "Both, please!"

We all had the same as Dad.

Another lady dressed in a similar way followed. She served us noodles and little pots of sauces.

It was a lovely evening, and we enjoyed the meal and the view as the sun lowered its head behind the mountains in the distance.

We returned to the house, and Mum made tea for everyone.

I drank my tea and looked out towards the river, feeling very lucky indeed to have a magical camper van.

"Thanks, Nifty," I whispered quietly and raised my cup to toast him.

Chapter Eighteen
Visiting Everest

Everyone was already up by the time I awoke in our house in the trees. I wandered out to the veranda, and Mum poured me a cup of tea. We sat quietly and I think we were all taking the time to reflect on Grandad's story.

A new day was in front of us, and what would this bring?

We dressed in long sleeve shirts and long trousers, which was advised in the welcoming notice in the house. Mosquitoes were everywhere, and I for one, didn't want them sucking on my blood!

Once we were all sorted, we walked to the dining room and sat at our sunken table.

Ladies were busy moving from one table to another, and they soon got to us.

They knelt down to our level and showed us the small packs of cereals. We picked what we wanted and put them in our bowls.

They brought small individual jugs of milk and pots with tea in them for each of us.

Once we finished our cereal, we were asked if we'd like some scrambled egg on toast, and they brought lots of fresh fruit to our table. Dad and I went for the scrambled egg, but Elizabeth and Mum had fruit.

An elephant came out of the tall grass with its trunk swinging to make a path. A man sat on its neck just behind the ears of the massive animal. Others followed.

"I'm going to get the cameras," Elizabeth called, and she climbed out of her seat and ran to the house.

I just stayed rooted to the spot as more and more elephants appeared from the grass.

Elizabeth returned with the cameras and the sound of all of our shutters broke the silence.

"Oh, George, take that one with its trunk in the air...Ooh get that one with the baby elephant." Mum yelled out instruction after instruction and Dad simply laughed and kept clicking.

The elephants lined up, and some of the other guests left the dining room and went down towards the waiting elephants.

The first elephant was stood next to a platform. We watched as a man and woman scaled the steps to the top. When she got to the platform, a man helped her on top of the elephant. They turned the elephant around and the man sat in the seat beside her, both behind its big ears.

The rest of the people did the same, and they then walked in single file towards the long grass and river.

I looked at Dad and hoped he could see what I wanted without my saying anything.

"All right, you don't have to ask. If there are spaces, we'll do it."

I grinned and Elizabeth gave me a high five, but Mum didn't seem quite as enthusiastic.

As we left our table and walked into the reception area, Dad went over to Batsa behind the desk. After a brief conversation, he returned.

"The elephants only do these rides twice a day,

morning and early evening. It has to be booked in advance, and obviously, we didn't know about it so we didn't book."

I looked at Elizabeth and sighed. I really wanted to amble through the jungle on a massive elephant.

"However, *Nifty* booked for us, and we'll be on this evening's ride looking for tigers and rhinos."

Elizabeth and I cheered.

"Come on, then. Back to the house we go," said Dad.

"Are you the Short family?"

We stopped and turned around to find a man in a long flowing coat, loose baggy trousers, and a coloured shirt. He had what looked like slippers on his feet.

"I'm Ranjin. I'm your driver to take you to the airfield for your plane ride."

"Driver? Goodness. And to an airfield? What's this?" exclaimed Mum.

"Madam, it's for Mount Everest. You are booked for a flight this morning. Are you wishing to cancel it?"

"No, definitely not," said Dad. "We didn't know we had a booking. It must be part of our gift package. Do we need to bring anything or are we fine as we are?"

Go, Dad. His quick thinking was pretty amazing. If only Nifty could have given us a list of what it had booked!

"Nothing else is required other than you joining me in my Jeep, and I will take you to your appointment with the aircraft."

Dad motioned to follow him. "Let's go then, Short family!"

We followed Ranjin down some steps to his Jeep. He opened the doors, placed a wooden step by the opened door, and invited Mum to get in first. Elizabeth followed, then myself, and lastly Dad.

Once we'd settled in the Jeep, all belted up against who knew what, Ranjin started the vehicle.

He drove down the track away from our temporary home and then turned through the long grass going towards the river. When he got there, Ranjin drove straight down the slope of the bank and through the water to the other side. Luckily it wasn't too deep or I thought we might have to call Nifty to the rescue!

Ranjin drove on and we passed lots of flowering trees and large clumps of the tall grass. After about half an hour, we came out to a large field with very short grass. It looked good enough to be a golf course. But no. It was the airfield. It literally was a field!

"I will wait for you while you fly and return you to Tiger Lodge," Ranjin said as he opened the doors of the Jeep.

We got out with the help of the wooden step and a pilot came over to us.

"The Short family?" he asked.

"Yes, that's us," said Dad.

"Glad to meet you. The name's Reg, and I'll fly you around Everest and back. It's a nice clear day so you'll get lots of amazing photos. I'm an Aussie, been over here for a while now. Never get tired of the views in this country, and the people are really great."

"Great! Let's go," I said.

"Have any of you been in a small plane like this before?"

"No. This is our first time for travelling abroad, and we've never flown."

"Strewth! So how did you get here? By boat?"

"By camper van actually," said Mum and gave us a wink.

"You drove? I take my hat off to you all. That's

some way you have come. You are from the UK, aren't you?"

"We are, indeed. Now, Reg, can we get going on our big adventure?" asked Dad.

"Sure. Just go careful up the steps here." He indicated the movable steps. "And remember to duck your head as you go in."

We all climbed in and sat in seats opposite each other. There was room for more people, but Reg followed us in, pulled the door shut and locked it. Our own private flight!

"It's very small, isn't it?" asked Mum.

"It's big enough for what we need, Mrs Short," Reg replied. "Okay, folks, buckle up and let's get on our way. I'll fly around Everest one way then turn the other way. Once we're on a level, you can leave your seat and take photos from any window. If, once we have our required height, one of you would like to look out from the front of the aircraft, you're welcome to do so. But when I let you know we're on our way back, I want you in your seats and buckled up."

I felt the plane move and looked out of the window to see the grass runway racing past us, and then we were going up. It was all so quick.

"Oh, boy, isn't this great?" I called out over the noise of the plane. "Our first flight and such amazing views."

Reg turned the plane and we saw the elephants below us as the plane pulled around and flew up the valley, climbing all the time.

After twenty minutes or so, Reg called out on the speakers, "Everest is in front of us now. If one of you'd like to come forward for a look-see, you can take it in turns."

Dad went first and took some photos, then

Elizabeth went next, then me. Mum sat with her seat belt on.

"Why don't you go up to the front and see the mountain range with Everest in the distance?" asked Dad.

"I don't understand how these things stay up," said Mum, "and why we don't fall from the sky."

"Come on. Be brave, Wendy. Here, take my hand, and I'll take you to the co-pilot's seat," said Dad.

"The last time you said 'be brave' to me, George Short, I ended up without a bra on. I'm not going there again!"

Dad laughed, and Elizabeth and I joined in. She went up to the front and sat next to Reg. It made me quite proud to see her being so courageous and facing her fears.

"Sit down, folks, please, but two stay on the left side where Everest will be," Reg said. "The other one will be able to catch the same view on the other side when we come about."

Elizabeth and I took a window to "catch the view."

Dad went to the right-hand side. Mum remained in the co-pilot's seat. We took lots of photos as we flew by. Then Reg turned the plane and returned to come past the mountain, now on the right-hand side.

After about half an hour, Reg called out that he was going to return back to the airfield, and Mum returned to a seat.

"Buckle up, folks," said Reg over the speakers.

And he started back the way we came. Still we took more photos of the mountains, all topped with snow and just as spectacular.

We slowly descended and soon we were touching down on the grass runway.

Once out of the plane, we said good-bye to Reg, and got in our Jeep taxi.

We returned to Tiger Lodge and thanked Ranjin for his help.

As we walked to our house on stilts, Batsa stopped us.

"Good afternoon, Sir, Madam. Would you like to have a buffet lunch on your veranda or shall we set out a table in the dining room?"

"Is it a light lunch?" Mum asked. "Because I've just been flying around Everest and much as I enjoyed it, I need my stomach to catch up with the rest of me!"

"It will be a cold buffet; cold meats, chicken, and salads," said Batsa.

"Then I'd like it on our veranda so we can enjoy the view as we eat."

"As you wish." And Batsa went on his way.

"Chicken. That sounds good doesn't it, Mum?" I said and gave her my best cheeky smile.

"I wonder if they've found our supply of chicken in Nifty," said Dad.

Mum just looked at us with a small smile on her

face, a clue in itself to stop teasing her!

We sat drinking our fruit juice and a short while later, the doorbell rang. Dad opened the door and two ladies pushed in two trolleys. They began to set a long table out in front of us. A very large bowl was placed in the middle, with other plates of food laid out. Jugs of tomato juice were placed on the table, along with orange and lime juice.

"Would you like wine or beer with your meal, Sir?" one of them asked.

"I'd love a local beer, please," said Dad.

A picnic on our veranda looking down over the trees and grass watching the river flow by. What more could I wish for?

Chapter Nineteen
A Family Reunited

We all had a little sleep after our meal. It was very hot, and it seemed we were all exhausted from doing very little. The table was cleared by the same ladies, and we spent some time relaxing on our beds and in the chairs.

At about four in the afternoon, we had a phone call asking us to come to the reception as the next elephant walk was due to start in a short while.

We pulled on our shoes again, brushed down our clothes, and then went to the reception.

"Please go down these steps, and your ride will arrive in a few minutes," Batsa said.

We went down, spoke to a few other people waiting, and it wasn't long before the elephants arrived. Everyone started taking photos! A few people were put on elephants before us but soon it was our turn to mount one. The man in charge put Elizabeth and I together to get a balanced load on each side.

The driver introduced himself as Girvesh. He nudged the ears of the elephant, and we moved forward clear of the platform. Now it was Mum and Dad's turn.

Mum climbed up first and Dad followed. She was

helped into her seat and secured in it. The elephant
was then turned, and Dad got in his seat. I took lots of
photos, hoping that I might see something funny like
my dad sliding out of the seat or the elephant blowing
water on them!

The elephants started to move away and we all
followed. We moved into the tall elephant grass but still
the grass tops were higher than us atop the elephants.

Slowly, we followed a path the elephant had made.
Suddenly we came out of the grass and our elephant
joined his friends in the water at the edge of the river.

Still following the others, our elephant walked
across the river. It went deep enough to come all the
way up to the its belly.

"Watch your feet don't get wet, Belle," I yelled
playfully. Belle grinned with delight and then we
climbed up the opposite bank.

As it walked along, our elephant wrapped its trunk

around great clumps of long bladed grass and pushed it into its mouth. I guess it needed plenty of energy to keep walking with Elizabeth and I on its back all night!

We passed through scrub-like bushes and long-leaved plants. Then the lead elephant stopped and the others drew alongside it.

In front of us was not just one rhino, but three!

Girvesh turned to us and put one finger to his mouth, indicating we should be quiet. Elizabeth and I took photos and saw Dad doing the same.

It was very hard to keep quiet; we were so excited and amazed at seeing wild animals. The first elephant started to move on, and we slowly got in line again.

I was glad the rhinos weren't bothered by the elephants at all. I don't think we would've outrun them!

We moved on and the trees became taller. Soon, we were enclosed by the foliage above us and around us—a jungle! There were vines hanging down and strange plants all around. I saw lots of monkeys moving through the trees.

Girvesh pointed out a snake looped around a tree branch. Birds were making a noise above us and butterflies of many colours and sizes flew by.

As we came out from the trees, Girvesh pointed to the bank on the opposite side, and we saw a tiger watching the elephants as they came from the jungle.

It must have decided that he couldn't mess with this many elephants, and as Mum and Dad's elephant came out of the jungle, it turned and strolled back up the bank and disappeared into the jungle. Phew!

I was keen to catch it on camera, but also a little scared. But what an amazing sight, and I struggled to contain my excitement.

"Steady there. Please do not jump around so much," said Girvesh.

"Sorry," I called forward to him and grinned at Elizabeth.

Once again, we followed the lead elephant and entered the jungle on the other side but away from the tiger. We made our way through the jungle then out onto the scrub and long grass area.

We crossed the river again, wandered up through the elephant grass, and arrived back at Tiger Lodge. We dismounted our elephant, and they were moved away.

Belle and I watched the elephants as they were led away, tails swaying side to side, before they disappeared under some trees.

We turned to each other, aware that we had just experienced an amazing thing that two weeks ago we could never have dreamed of.

"Well, little sister, first we fly in a plane in the morning, then in the afternoon we go trekking in the jungle on the back of an elephant. I don't think anything could top the day we have just had."

"Got to agree, big bro. It's been a wonderful experience."

It was beginning to get very dark as we went back to our lodge. I felt quite sticky from the heat, and we took it in turns to shower in nice cool water. Mum put on a caftan dress that the lodge provided and she looked really good in it.

We all went out onto the veranda, and Dad dropped the mosquito screens down. We quietly watched the last of the sunlight disappear.

Mum went over to Dad and sat on his lap. He wrapped his arms around her. "George, this has been such a whirlwind visit, but we've seen and done so much. I'd never left England before, and now here I am in Nepal. I've always been too scared and found reasons not to try anything new. I've never done anything amazing, but when we travelled along the mountain pass, I was just blown away at the beauty of it all. I was scared but thrilled at the same time."

"I think that goes for all of us, Wendy. We've seen some wonderful things in the last few days, and I bet it's opened their eyes to the world we live in. And I'm sure they would want more. I know I do."

"Yes," Elizabeth and I said almost at the same time.

Mum smiled. "None of us had ever been in a plane before. We knew about Mount Everest, but now we've actually seen it! What I'm saying is that all of this is down to Nifty, my grandad—uncle. I'd like to tell him that I forgive him and release his soul to return to his ashes."

"But, Mum, wouldn't the camper van just be an old broken-down thing if you did that?" I asked, a little panicked that we could lose our magical camper van so soon.

"It would, but we shouldn't be selfish," Mum said. "Grandad gave us this ability to say thank you but also to say sorry. I want to accept his gift, accept his being my uncle and not the grandad I knew, and forgive him with all my heart. If that means no more Nifty, then we'll all know that he's happy and at rest."

"Wendy, if that's your wish, then we'll support it. I'm glad you've settled your mind with your grandad-uncle issue. He *will* have peace, but most importantly to me, so will you."

Mum looked at us after she kissed Dad on his cheek. "Daniel?"

"I understand, Mum. I'll be sad to lose Nifty but if it makes you happy, that's what you should do. We only have Nifty because of your love for Grandad. We only went to see him once a year and then reluctantly."

"Elizabeth?"

"I agree with Daniel. I'd hate to walk home from here, so can you ask him to take us back first?"

Everyone couldn't help but laugh. Ever the practical one, my sister!

"Then I'm going to talk to Uncle Rowland alone. I'll tell him everything we've said." Mum looked at Elizabeth. "And I'll let him know of your request. But whatever he decides, we'll abide by it. We can always fly home; Uncle left us plenty of money too."

"We could donate all the food in it to Tiger Lodge," said Dad. "I'm sure they could use it."

Mum gave Dad a playful punch and got up from his lap.

She looked at us both, then moved to the door. Just as she was going to open it, the doorbell rang.

Mum opened the door and found a monk dressed in yellow stood outside the door.

"May I enter?" Yellow monk asked, as he waved around a bunch of sweet-smelling plants.

Mum moved away from the door and let him come in. She closed the door and Dad held her hand.

Yellow monk looked at all of us slowly. "I am required to convey to you a message of most importance. Your ancestor, our brother, has requested that you should be aware that he has listened to your discussion and your decision to release him from his penitence. He has been touched by all of your thoughts and your forgiveness of his foolishness. It is therefore our brother's wish to remain as part of your family as Nifty."

Mum began to cry, and I was very close to it. Even Dad looked to be struggling to hold back the tears and kept blinking and looking to the ceiling.

"You should know that our brother will always be able to join us. He will never be denied."

Mum rushed over to the yellow monk and hugged him. He looked surprised but smiled.

She let him go and stepped back. "I'm so overwhelmed by the thought that he finally wants to spend time with us. He's welcome in any form, just as he always was."

The yellow monk put his hands together, fingers pointed up, and bowed to us. "I must return now to my meditation. May your journey in your world always bring enlightenment," he said. He took the herbs from under his arm where he had placed them to bow to us. He went to the door and left without another word.

"Wait. I didn't say thank you." Mum rushed to the door, opened it, and stepped out. She came back in looking puzzled. "How strange. There's no sign of him."

I looked at Elizabeth. "More magic." She nodded.

"If he can come to the door only moments after

we'd just had our conversation about Nifty, I'm sure he'll already know how grateful we all are," said Dad. "I expect he went through some sort of doorway back to Nirvana, just like Nifty did."

"Can we all go down to Nifty?" I asked. "Grandad obviously likes the name. We could all say thank you. Then it'll be dinner time. I wonder if it'll be chicken?"

Mum laughed and gave me a gentle shove.

I led the way down to thank Nifty, our magical camper van: a true member of our family.

Chapter Twenty
Returning Home

We spent a little time talking to Nifty and told him of our first flight in an aircraft, how we saw Mount Everest, and the ride on an elephant, and the sighting of a tiger and the rhinos.

I didn't care if anyone saw us talking to him.

Finally, we all touched Nifty and said thank you.

We went back up the stairs and into the dining area. We waved to the people who'd been on the elephant trek with us, went to our sunken table, and settled in for food.

As before, the ladies came and placed jugs of juice on the table, and I had tomato juice. Fruit was placed in the middle in a big bowl. They brought large bowls of mixed vegetables with steam rising from them. Then came the sweet potatoes with paprika sprinkled over them. The next dish was chicken cuts with a honey glaze, and Mum grinned as she looked at me.

The ladies served everything, and our plates were soon piled high. We even had gravy, but it was nothing like Mum's.

We ate quickly—I think all that crying had made everyone hungry!

A local dance demonstration was being provided

for our entertainment, so we made our way to the
reception area, cameras at the ready. Large moths
fluttered around the lights in many bright colours, some
looking as if they had camouflage. One was green and
its wings looked like leaves from a tree.

It was a lovely evening, everyone was dressed in
very colourful outfits, but I enjoyed the strange music
and dances. I didn't understand the singing or what they
were doing, but I was glad I'd seen it. Mum had a glass
of the local coconut liquor and said it was very nice,
but she probably wouldn't have it again. I guess this
was Mum being a little more relaxed about trying new
things.

I was tired by the time we returned to the lodge.
Dad made a point of thanking Batsa and the lovely
ladies who'd served our meals for us. I heard Batsa ask if
we wanted any help with the suitcases in the morning—
it looked like our big adventure was coming to an end.

***

Mum was busy making tea for us as we drifted into
the lounge the next morning. Dad was the last one to
appear and sat down next to me on the veranda. As
we looked out over the elephant grass to the distant
mountains that I'd come to love as my normal morning
view, I remembered that it was the day we were going
home. I felt a little deflated but at least Nifty was
sticking around and we'd get to go to lots of other new
places.

I watched a big bird, maybe a buzzard or a vulture,
circling around on a thermal as the day warmed up.

"It's been an incredible trip, Daniel," said Dad.

"I've loved every minute of it," I said.

Dad and I sat for quite a time watching the bird

and sipping our tea until Mum reminded us that we should get dressed and start gathering things together.

Once we'd finished, we packed all our things into the bags we'd brought them in. Mum folded our clothes and placed them in the suitcases.

"These can just go into Nifty as they are. I'll wash them when we get home."

We sorted everything out, made sure we had all the leads for our cameras, phones, and iPads, and once Mum was satisfied, we started to take things to Nifty.

Dad checked around the house for any odd thing we might've missed and locked the house. We all walked down to the reception.

"All packed up to leave," said Dad to Batsa and gave him our key.

"Thank you for staying in Tiger Lodge. Enjoy your breakfast and have a safe journey home."

We went into the dining room, sat for the last time at our low table, and ate our breakfast. Once we had finished, we said a few good-byes to the guests we'd spoken to and went down the stairs to Nifty.

I got in, feeling very sad that this adventure was at an end and settled in my seat.

Mum got in the front with Dad and closed the door. "Okay, Nifty, let's keep up appearances. Drive away, then when no one can see us, work your magic, please," she said.

Nifty reversed out from under the reception and then started driving down the track. I was looking out of the window at the tall grasses as we went on our way, marvelling that I'd been to such a place. I couldn't wait to tell Garry all about it—well, maybe not *all* about it. As we rounded a corner and the grass was surrounding us, Nifty stopped and began to shake. The grass faded to become our garage.

We unloaded our things and everything went into the house.

Mum smiled as we brought the chicken back in, and she told us she would make a meal for us this evening using some of it.

Once we'd emptied Nifty, we all said a little thank you to him before going in to sort everything out.

After Mum had put a wash in, we sat in the lounge to talk.

"One thing I'm sure about, I won't be taking any frozen chicken with us on our next adventure. I'll leave it to Nifty to organise."

We laughed, then I had a thought. "How would we organise something like that again. We went to Nepal for a reason, but what about other places that Nifty hasn't been to?"

"The same thought had occurred to me," said Mum. "And I don't know what the solution is."

"Well, Nifty seems to be able to listen to our conversations," Dad said. "If we wanted to go somewhere, we'd research the place and figure out what we'd need for that holiday."

"That's okay," I said, "but what if Mum just said something like, I think we will just slip down to the shops and go to Iceland. We could find ourselves in the real Iceland! It's not the worst thing that could happen and I wouldn't mind a drive around Iceland for the scenery, but you get what I mean."

"Daniel has a point," said Mum. "He does take what I say very literally! Remember how he left your Dad at the house and just brought us home?!"

I smiled. "That *was* funny, though."

"I think we should make some plans," said Elizabeth.

"Like a bucket list? Now that's a very good idea,"

said Mum. "Let's each get a piece of paper and write our own wish list, then we can compare notes and see what's possible."

Dad got up, dug out a pad of note paper and passed a sheet to each of us.

"Are there any rules?" he asked.

"I don't think there needs to be. The obvious thing to remember is that Nifty isn't a time machine so no travelling back in time," said Mum.

"So touring Iceland isn't out of the question then?" I asked.

"That seems perfectly reasonable to me and given how Nifty organised our time in Nepal, that would probably be easy for him!"

I thought for a while, and everyone was scribbling away as ideas came.

Mum stopped to hang the washing in the garden, then she returned.

"It's blowing quite a bit out there. If it doesn't rain, I should get a couple of washes done today."

She sat looking at her list, then picked up the pen, and continued writing.

"How many ideas have you got, Daniel?" asked Elizabeth.

"I've got four or maybe five. One idea I'm not sure of."

"I've got seven, but I think Mum won't like one."

"My list is the longest then," said Dad. "But some are in the UK."

"No matter what's on our list, it's fun thinking about these places, whether they happen or not," said Mum.

"Well, shall we do the rounds and talk about what we'd all like to do? And if the vote is yes, we tick it. If it's no, we cross it off," said Dad.

Dad read out his list first, and we said yes to quite a few. Elizabeth went next and called out her ideas. She had put Iceland down, so when it was voted for, I ticked it on my list. I went next and only one other idea was ticked. Then I came to my wild idea.

"I wondered if it'd be a good idea to ask Nifty to take us to the places that he's been to. We could ask for say, an architectural visit, for a couple of days, something like we've just done." I shuffled to the edge of my seat, getting more excited about what I'd like us to do. "I was thinking about how we could talk to him, too. If we said that two toots on Nifty's horn means 'yes' and one means 'no,' then we could ask him questions."

"Daniel, that's a wonderful idea. As long as the answers are yes or no, that will work brilliantly."

"Thanks, Mum," I said. "But it would be a little bit of a mystery tour, and you said you wanted to plan them all out. This way, we wouldn't know where we're going until we got there."

We talked about this for a lot longer and then asked Mum for her ideas.

Some were ticked, some discarded, and then she also came out with a strange idea.

"I've always had a dream of going to Venice on the Orient Express. We now have some money thanks to Uncle. I'd like to use some to make that dream come true."

Dad put his arm around Mum and pulled her into a hug. "And I've always wanted to make that dream come true. We should absolutely go, Wendy."

We broke up our discussions, and Mum asked us to bring the washing in as she prepared dinner.

As the evening came towards bedtime, I went upstairs wondering where we'd be going next in Nifty, our wonderful family camper van!

Chapter Twenty-One
One Toot or Two

I ambled down the next morning. The weather outside looked brighter than I felt. Mum was making tea and within a few moments, thrust a mug in front of me.

"There we are, Daniel, your usual pick-me-up."

I thanked her with a grunt and held my mug tightly as if my life depended on it. I stared into the distance.

A voice cut into my comatose state, and I became aware that Dad had joined me. "Sorry? Did you say something, Dad?"

"I said 'Daniel, did you sleep well?' but judging by your lack of response, you did."

"Sorry, Dad. I haven't quite woken up yet."

"Drink your tea, Daniel. Your dad's had two while you were in your morning dream state!" said Mum.

I drank my tea and as I finished, Mum took the mug and refilled it. This time I was able to improve on my first effort and managed a "Ta," as it was passed to me.

I looked at Dad who grinned at me.

"Any chance that you will get dressed today?" he asked.

I nodded, seeing that he and Mum were already dressed. Elizabeth came in and said good morning to everyone.

"Is he with us yet?" she asked Mum as she pointed to me.

"I'm getting there," I said. "But I fail to see how you can all be so wide awake at this time in the morning," I said and yawned.

"It's gone seven o'clock, Daniel. You'd be up and having breakfast under normal circumstances," said Mum.

I finished my tea and got up to go and get dressed.

Elizabeth stepped in front of me. "Your idea about talking to Nifty was a good one, Daniel. I thought about some ways we could ask the general questions, and I am sure this could work." She grinned. "You do have the occasional good idea, big brother."

I returned the grin. "Yeah, right." I turned and left the room to go up to get dressed.

When I returned, I sat once again at the breakfast table and my third mug of tea was passed to me.

"It's a very nice day today and we thought we would walk down to Uncle's house and see how everything was coming on."

"I would like to download my photos of Nepal," Elizabeth said.

"Okay. If you'd like to stay here to do that, your dad can stay here, and I will stroll down. Do you want to join me, Daniel?"

"No, thanks. I want to compare shots with Elizabeth."

We ate our cereals and then once the breakfast things were cleared, Mum went on her way. Elizabeth and I went upstairs to get our cameras before meeting up in the lounge at the family computer. Elizabeth pulled up a chair and sat beside me.

Dad watched us for a moment before he picked up

the paper, followed by a pen he had on a table by his side and immersed himself in a crossword.

"Do you want to do it?" she asked as she removed her memory stick.

"No, you do it. You're more awake than I am."

She plugged each of the sticks into the computer, highlighted the photos, and dragged them into a blank folder. We checked through them and discarded any that were out of focus.

"Can I have some of yours in my folder? I love that one of Mum on the elephant."

Elizabeth smiled widely. "Only if I can have some of yours."

"Of course you can."

And so we swapped some photos into each other's folders.

"Shall we print some out for Mum to show the WI ladies?" Belle asked.

"Great idea! She'll love that."

We sat back, satisfied that we both had a brilliant file of photos of our all too brief time in Nepal.

"Saving the files like this is okay but sometime in the near future, we should make a picture show of them, then put them on a memory stick to be played on the TV or through any PC."

Elizabeth was printing a few more photos to show her friends when Mum came in.

Dad put the newspaper down and looked up at Mum. "How's it going down there, then?" he asked.

"The house is looking very nice now. It'll be finished in two or three days' time. I think it's time to ring the estate agents and get them to view it to put it on the market."

"Elizabeth has printed a few photos for you to show your friends in the WI."

"Oh, what a lovely thought, Elizabeth. I'll put them with my bag now to take next time I go." She picked up the photos and went upstairs.

Dad returned to his crossword.

"I'm going to talk to Nifty. Want to come?" I asked Belle.

"I'm with you, big brother," she said.

We went out through the kitchen and opened the side garage door. I stepped in and stopped immediately causing Elizabeth to bump into me. She stepped around me but then she skidded to a halt too.

"Nifty?"

"It must be," I said.

"But how?"

"And why?" I said.

The cause of our amazement was the vehicle in front of us. We were looking at a pale blue, pristine camper van. Not a sign of rust, it gleamed as if it has just rolled off the production line.

We walked up to it and then around to the front. I touched the bonnet gently. "Is this still you, Nifty?" I asked.

Two toots on the horn echoed around the garage.

"You did it, Daniel! Nifty's talking to us!"

Elizabeth turned to Nifty. "You've got a brand-new look, Nifty. But why?"

Nothing! And I knew exactly why. "Sorry, Nifty. You can't answer that kind of question, can you?"

One toot.

"Okay. Now let me ask one you can answer yes or no to. Did you change your appearance for us?"

Two toots.

"Yes! He said yes!" Elizabeth laughed.

"Did you hear my suggestion yesterday, Nifty, even when you were out here and we were indoors?"

Two toots.

"Goodness, we need to be careful what we say about you, Nifty."

Two toots.

"Could we go to some of the places you went to as Grandad?"

Two toots.

"Would you like to talk to Mum, Nifty?"

Two toots.

"I'll get Mum, Danny. You stay with Nifty." Elizabeth hurried out of the garage.

"Rather than Grandad or Uncle Rowland, can we go on calling you Nifty?"

Two toots.

Mum and Dad came in. Both stopped as I had causing Elizabeth to collide into them.

"What's happened?" asked Dad as Elizabeth squeezed back into the garage.

"We've been talking to Nifty," said Elizabeth.

"This is Nifty?" asked Mum as she motioned to the immaculate camper van.

Two toots.

"Two toots? Is that yes or no, Daniel?"

"Nifty gives us two toots for yes and one toot for no. So he said yes."

"Good grief. We can talk to Nifty, just as you thought, Daniel."

"You might want to know that Nifty can hear what we say even when we're in the house."

"Everything, Nifty?" asked Mum.

Two toots.

"That's embarrassing to say the least."

"Especially after last night," said Dad.

"But, Mum, if Nifty hadn't listened to us last night, he wouldn't have known we'd try to talk to him. Why would that be embarrassing?"

"Um, well, Daniel. Dad and I may have said a few personal words to each other, like I love you and things like that. It's embarrassing to think that Nifty could listen to us."

Ewww, as if I don't know what you're talking about. I turned to Nifty. "Nifty, can you stop listening to Mum and Dad when they are in the house kissing and stuff?"

"Daniel!"

Two toots.

"There. You can kiss as much as you want now. Nifty won't be listening."

Mum had changed to a red colour, so I guess she was embarrassed.

"Daniel Short, you really are a one. And what do you mean by 'and stuff?'"

"Oh, come on, Mum. We did it in biology at school. I know I didn't arrive by a stork!"

Mum's colour deepened.

"Let's move on, shall we? What have you two found out so far?" Dad asked.

"Nifty wants to be called Nifty, rather than Grandad or Uncle. We can go to places he has been to before with no problems. What else? Oh yes, he changed his appearance for us. Rather smart, I think. In fact, quite Nifty!"

"You have been busy, haven't you?" Dad looked impressed.

Mum moved to Nifty and touched the bonnet.

"You know the places you've been to, but we don't so I have some questions. Firstly, did you go to cultural cities to wander around?"

Two toots.

"Did you go to Berlin?"

One toot.

"Can one of you write the answers down, please? It will help us get ideas for short visits."

"I'll get paper and a pen." Dad disappeared out of the garage.

"How about Barcelona?"

Two toots.

"Lovely. I've always wanted to go there."

Nifty's front doors opened and his headlights flashed on and off.

"No, no, Nifty. Not just yet, but maybe soon. My goodness we are going to have some lovely times together."

Two toots and the doors closed as Dad returned waving his paper.

"Put Barcelona down as a yes," Elizabeth said to him.

Mum went on with a list of cities that she and Dad wanted to visit.

I asked about Disney World but got only one toot. *Well that's a real bummer.*

Mum then changed to countries and started with Egypt.

Two toots.

The questions and toots kept coming, and Dad wrote them all down.

"I need more paper!"

I rushed in, picked up another sheet from the printer's stock, and went back to Dad. The list grew, and at last Mum stopped.

"Thank you, Nifty. We have a lot to go through. Are you happy to take us to all these places?"

The front doors opened and Nifty tooted twice.

"We'll go in and see how many places on this list are on the list we made last night. We'll talk to you again soon."

We left our bright, shiny new camper van and went back inside.

What a surprise this had been. Now we had to prioritise.

Mum made a chicken curry and cleared another lot of pre-cooked chicken. I wondered if the chicken would ever run out. Then our conversation turned to our next trip with Nifty. Everyone agreed on a beach holiday for three or four days.

"I'd like to go snorkelling. I did some before in Devon on one of our holidays, but I didn't see a lot. But it was good practice," I said.

Once a type of holiday was decided, we went back into the garage and asked Nifty if he could take us to somewhere warm with white sand and clear blue waters suitable for snorkelling.

Nifty didn't respond for a moment but then flashed his lights.

"Do you know somewhere like that?" Dad asked.

Two toots.

"Is it on our list?"

One toot.

A mystery place, and if it turned out that it was half as good as the Nepal, we'd be very happy.

"Can you make the arrangements, Nifty, say from tomorrow for four days?"

Two toots.

Summer sun, here we come!

Chapter Twenty-Two
The Secret Beach

So it was that today we were packing light summer clothes into suitcases and grabbing our cameras and iPads ready to go. Dad found his mobile phone that had somehow climbed out of his pocket, and Mum reminded us all to take our swimming gear. She'd nipped to the corner shop after dinner to get some suntan lotion. We were soon ready and raring to go.

"We are taking bottles of water with us but no food, and before anyone dares to make any comment, no, I'm not packing any chicken, cooked or not!" said Mum.

We all smiled but said nothing.

Everyone piled into Nifty, and Mum asked him to take us on our mystery holiday.

I could almost feel everyone's excitement as we waited for the shaking to start. We looked out of the windows to see our garage dissolve and turn into an aqua blue sea.

We had arrived but to where? If Nifty had turned into a boat again, then we must've been on a very calm sea.

"I'll open a door and look out. I don't want any of you dropping into the sea," said Dad.

He opened the door and looked down. "I'll come around to you."

He walked around the front of Nifty and opened Mum's door.

"We're on stilts over the water," said Dad, "and Nifty has changed on the outside. He's a wooden house on stilts with a walkway all around. Nifty's now got a straw roof and his wheels are on the side. His radiator grill is on one end of the house. There are other houses in the row, and we're at the end of the boardwalk."

Mum got out, and we got out the same way because Nifty had stopped us using the other exit. I shut the door behind me.

Nifty shook and when we looked inside again, the camper van interior had changed to a house.

I opened the door and looked in. We had a very spacious lounge with one side looking out to sea. As I stepped inside, Dad came around to the door I was looking through.

"We have a deck area with four easy chairs to use. We even have a pull-out table!"

"Everything's changed inside too, Dad. Look at this. It's really top notch."

"Nifty's done it again, Daniel."

"He certainly has. I haven't explored the rest of the house but look over there," I said as I pointed to a corner that had steps going down.

We moved across to it and saw that it led down to a platform under our Nifty house with water about a foot deep over it. We could walk down the steps and just start swimming from the platform out into the sea!

As we explored the house, Dad claimed the large bedroom. Elizabeth and I got the next two smaller bedrooms and both had sea views.

Our final find was the all-important bathroom.

"There's no kitchen," said Dad as we returned to the lounge.

I pointed across the room. "There's a work surface over there and the kettle is on it."

"Mugs?" asked Dad.

Nifty opened a panel and mugs, tea, coffee, and biscuits were all in the hidden cupboard. Mum and Elizabeth came in.

"We've been exploring," Mum said.

"Oh, and what have you found?" Dad asked.

"Well, Elizabeth and I walked along the walkway that joins all of the rest of the houses like our one. We're on the end of the rank; the largest one I might add," she said with a little pride.

"And…" said Dad.

"We're on Moon Island in the Seychelles!"

"The Seychelles? Where is that?" I asked.

"The Indian Ocean, Daniel. It's a cluster of islands that are threatened by global warming," said Elizabeth.

159

"We covered this in one of our lessons a few weeks ago. Didn't you do this in my year at school?"

"I vaguely remember something about it, but Seychelles was just a word to me. It didn't seem likely that I'd ever go there, or so I thought. Now I *am* here. How wrong can someone be?"

"We met a very nice couple. Mr and Mrs Archer, they were called. They asked us when we arrived and what sea cabin we were in. We told them we got here about half an hour ago and where we were."

"What did they say to that?"

"That's the strange thing, George. They said we must be in one of the private owner's cabins. I just said they were right."

"One of the private owner's cabins? Do you think we've taken over someone's home and Nifty has morphed it?"

"I have no idea, George, but we could see quite a few of these walkways going out into the sea and similar houses like ours are on the end of each walkway."

"Nifty, have you morphed yourself into another person's home?" Dad asked.

One toot.

"Have you created a new house and attached yourself to the walkway, so no one will know we are an additional house?" asked Dad.

Two toots.

"Nifty, you're so clever. Thank you."

The lights in the house flashed on and off.

"I think Nifty is enjoying these adventures with us just as much as we are."

Two toots.

We all burst out laughing and the lights inside our house went on and off also, as if Nifty was laughing.

Once we calmed down, we decided to explore the island. We changed into our swimming costumes and put sun tan lotion on ourselves—Mum put it on our backs. We all put on hats and sand shoes.

We walked to the end of the walkway onto the island. It was still a walkway, but it was stone instead of wood. Palm trees sheltered us a little, but the sun still came through as the fronds waved in the breeze. There were orchids all around us and plants that looked like the ones we'd found in the house.

I stopped looking at the plant, then said to the others who'd stopped and were looking at me, "Do you think Nifty, when he was Grandad, got some of the plants from here? This one here," I said pointing to it, "looks very much like one that was in the plant room."

They moved back to me and stared at the plant.

"Well, it is a very close likeness, Danny. Maybe he did."

"It's very observant of you to notice it, Danny. I'd just passed it by."

We continued our walk once again, but I noticed we were all now studying the plants a little more as we passed.

Birds chattered above us, and as we looked up, we caught glimpses of them passing from tree to tree with their bright and beautiful colours flashing in the sun.

We came to a junction with a sign that had Moon Island written on the top. Under it was a sign to the reception area and restaurant being straight on. Left would take us to Ray Beach and the sports centre and Coral Bay was to the right.

"Interesting names. Coral Bay suggests we might get some snorkelling in. Ray Beach could refer to the shape or actual stingrays being near the shore."

I liked the last idea.

"Which way then?" asked Mum.

"Let's go to the reception to see if they know we're here. You never know what Nifty might have already arranged."

We followed the path under the trees and came to a long building. It was built in wood and seemed to be at the edge of this side of the island. We followed the signs for the reception, walked in, and went up to the counter where a very pretty young lady stood.

"Good morning, Sir. How can I help you?"

"My name is George Short, and this is my family," said Dad as he motioned to us.

"Just one moment, Sir." She flicked through some paperwork behind her.

"Yes, Sir, we have your booking here. You're on a short booking in one of the private cabins, and you've paid for the restaurant services in advance. These are your family's restaurant passes."

She passed over four cards with our names on them. "Please show them prior to taking your seat. The restaurant is a buffet, and you can help yourself to as much or as little as you want." She passed over some more paperwork to Dad.

"If you would be good enough to read these events and indicate if you'd like to participate in any of them, we will see what we can arrange. We have your visitor's permit. It came in today by fax."

"Wonderful," said Dad.

Good old, Nifty. You've done it again: everything arranged and food provided. Lovely.

"This is the map of the island and the opening times for our restaurant."

Dad took the sheet of paper. "Thank you."

"Welcome to Moon Island, Sir. I hope you and your family have a lovely stay."

"Can I look at the list of events please, Dad?" I asked.

"Sure, Daniel," he said as he passed it to me.

I glanced at it, then gave it back to Dad.

"Anything catch your eye?" asked Dad.

"Not at first glance, although there's something here about feeding stingrays," I replied.

"Okay, we can study this a little later," Dad said.

We left the reception and retraced our steps to the crossing. We walked along the path, nodding to other people as we passed them. After a ten-minute stroll, we came to the sports centre and Coral Bay.

The sports centre was for all kinds of water sports and I bubbled with excitement when I saw they included snorkelling. We asked about it and told the guy there that we had our own snorkelling gear. Nifty must've been a boy scout when he was younger because he'd thought of everything. The man pointed along the bay and said the coral section was good all the way along it. He warned us not to touch any coral and he told us that the red and yellow coral was called fire coral.

"Thanks for the warning," Dad said. "What can you tell us about Ray Beach?"

"Oh, that's named after the stingrays that come in on an evening. The restaurant saves the fish heads and tails, and we hand feed them every evening. Our clients like to join in, so we show them how to do it without the rays taken a finger as extra protein!"

"Oh, Dad, we've got to do that. It sounds awesome," said Elizabeth.

"Please can we, Dad?" I pleaded, "This must be the 'event' I spoke about earlier on at reception."

"We'll see," Dad said before he thanked the man.

We headed back to Nifty and told him all about the

stingrays. We were all so grateful for another amazing trip.

We all drank some water then stripped down to our swimming costumes. Dad lifted the thick clear lid that covered the stairs and walked down the steps, and onto a platform.

The water was lovely and warm, and in no time at all, we were swimming out from under the house. We could see all sorts of fish below us and a lot were under the other cabins on stilts.

When we'd had enough, we swam back to our platform, wrapped ourselves in our beach towels, and trotted up the stairs. We went to our bedrooms to dry and change.

"All that swimming's made me super hungry," I said.

"Then let's go eat."

Dad led the way to the restaurant. On the way, Mum greeted a couple, and she introduced them as the people she and Elizabeth had met earlier.

"You know, I can't recall seeing your cabin at the end of the walkway. I said to Mr Archer that it was as if it just suddenly appeared."

Dad chuckled. "Oh dear, we're going to have to confess to you, then. You're right. We're actually alien time travellers collecting specimens to take back to our planet."

Mrs Archer laughed but it seemed a little nervous. "I hope you're joking."

"Indeed I am...but we must leave you now. We're off to sample some Earth food. Goodbye for now."

I put my hand over my mouth and tried not to laugh. Who knew Dad was so funny?

"George, you should be ashamed of yourself. That poor woman wasn't sure if you meant it or not," Mum said after we'd walked away.

"Just imagine her shock when she sees the empty space after we leave. Oh, sorry, did I say space?!"

We all laughed and even Mum giggled.

We had a nice light lunch at the restaurant then returned and walked to the beach. We laid in the shade of the palm trees and occasionally went for a swim.

As the sun began to slowly set, we packed up and strolled back to our Nifty cabin. We showered and changed and went back to the restaurant.

After a very nice meal, we went down to Ray Beach. People were standing around on the water's edge, and some were up to their ankles in the water. Two men came down to the beach carrying a big bucket between them. They called everyone in before one went chest deep into the water and threw some bits of fish into the water.

He walked back in, and we saw a big black triangle shape come closer to the shore. Another long thin tail broke the water's surface as a ray took some of the scraps. One of the men placed a fish head in his flat hand and slowly lower his hand into the water to demonstrated how to feed the rays.

A big ray came up to his hand covered it, and then swam away, and the fish head was gone. We all had a go except Mum.

"There's no way I'm putting my hand in a huge great fish's mouth," she said.

I walked into the water almost up to my knees and different types of rays swam around us. I could see them easily through the clear water.

"Stand still, young man," one of the men said to me.

"Okay." I did as he asked but was already wondering why.

"Good lad. Now they will come to you. Don't be scared; they won't bite you."

I stood still, and as I looked in front of me, a dark spotted shape and another large black triangle started to swim towards me. Both swam around me, brushing their fins against my legs as they went by.

Awesome!

It was a bit scary. The big black one looked very menacing, but it was so cool to be brushed by two different rays.

Belle hadn't come deep enough to do the same, but small fish were swimming around her.

When I came out alone I told Mum and Dad about it who'd been watching from the shoreline.

"It was great. They just stroked my legs as they passed by. The black ray was a bit like sandpaper, but the spotted ray was as smooth as silk."

"Quite an experience then, Daniel," said Mum.

"Absolutely, and all thanks to Nifty."

Our time ended on the beach once the scraps had been eaten, and we went back to go to bed.

What a wonderful day it had been.

Chapter Twenty-Three
Another Day

We woke early, and Mum made tea. Dad, still in his pyjamas, was outside on the decking. I went out to join him with my wake-me-up life-saver mug of tea. Not that I was feeling quite so much in a fog as I usually do.

I guess I was still buzzing from the rays yesterday evening. I could still see them coming towards me as I shut my eyes.

Dad stared out at the water, and he looked deep in thought.

"You know, Daniel, I could get used to this life."

"Travelling around the world?"

"Yes, that, but also the unexpected places like this. Your grandad must've seen some incredible sights and done some things."

Two toots.

"Are you two talking to Nifty?" asked Mum as she put her head around the door.

"No, Wendy, but he seems to be listening anyway."

Elizabeth came out to join us, and Mum brought out a big tea pot for us to replenish our mugs. We all sat in our pyjamas looking out to the sea.

"I was just saying to Daniel that Nifty must have

seen some incredible sights and done amazing things."

"And," I added, "how easy we could get used to doing this."

Mum smiled and reached for Dad's mug. "So you want to become a beach bum, do you, George?"

Dad glared at me and I shrugged. "What? You said it, not me."

"Never mind, my darling, George. Why not settle for being a part time beach bum?"

She passed him his mug of tea, and gave him a smile, as she filled my mug for my second drink. Dad smirked and sipped his tea.

"I thought we could start the day with breakfast and then go up to Coral Bay to let you snorkel," said Mum.

"That sounds like a plan," said Dad.

"I could try the new underwater case for my camera. I've not tried it in the swimming pool," Belle said.

Dad put his cup down. "Right, people. I'm going to get my swimmers on. Let's get ready."

We all finished our drinks and went to our rooms to change.

It was starting to get warmer as we walked together along the walkway from our Nifty cabin.

"Oh, I'm glad I caught you," said Mrs Archer.

"Good morning. I hope this morning finds you well."

She raised her eyebrow at Dad.

"Well, it finds me confused, Mr Short. I took this photo before I met you looking up the board walk towards your cabin. And, look, it's not there. Yet as you can see, it's clearly there now."

Dad looked at the display on the back of Mrs Archer's camera and passed it along for us all to take a look.

"Mrs Archer—"

"You can call me Martha."

"Martha," Dad continued. "There are two possibilities to explain this photo. The first one is your confusion. Could it be that you wandered up one of the other walkways and took that. I think each one is slightly different."

Martha shook her head. "No. It was definitely this one. Look, there's my husband outside the door of our cabin."

"Then it has to be the second reason," said Dad.

She started to back away from us all.

"You really are aliens," she said.

Dad laughed. "No, Martha, nothing like that. It must be a problem with the camera."

"Really? How so?" she asked and took a step back towards Dad.

He pointed to her camera. "I notice you've got a model that the company recalled a short time ago. Its focal range was not very good, something to do with it blanking out sections in the viewer."

"I didn't know about that. And you think that could be the problem?"

"Well, it'd be easy to check," said Dad.

"How do I do that?"

"Why don't you stand on this walkway and line up your camera in the exact spot you think you stood in to take this photo and take another photo."

"That makes sense. I could compare it to this one," she said.

She walked back to the area she must have thought she'd stood in before and we followed, not wishing to be in the photo.

"Line up the photo as best as you can to the

original, and when you're happy, take another photo. I'll bet that you won't be able to see our Nifty cabin in your photo."

She lined up her camera and took the shot.

"Let's have a look at it, then," said Dad.

She put the camera onto playback and looked at the photo.

"Why it's not there! Goodness. Thank you for pointing that out to me. You don't know how pleased I am to know you're not really aliens!"

"I think you'll find that no matter how close you get to our cabin now, because of your camera's residual memory, it just won't show up. Just think, you may have photos of the beach with one palm tree missing. Well, I think we should get our breakfast and get on with our day. Goodbye, Martha."

We moved away and Mum laughed. "How do you manage to come out with these sneaky ideas, George, with such a straight face?"

"Well, Nifty is always listening, and I hoped he'd follow my train of thought. She could see Nifty, but if she couldn't photo him, then it must be a mechanical problem. She will spend the day now going around retaking her beach photos to see if a palm tree is missing or a rock has gone."

"But, George, that poor woman will think she is stupid by the time she finishes her photo shoot."

"Well, Wendy, it was that or we declare we are time travellers. I don't think that would be a good idea."

We went to the restaurant and had our meal, then went to Coral Bay. We put on our masks and goggles and went into the water. We swam out to the reef and I marvelled at the amount of fish around it.

I saw a lion fish like I'd seen on TV, and now here it

was in front of me. There were long spikes sticking out amongst its wavy fins.

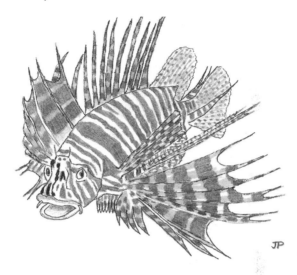

We snorkelled for quite some time, then swam back to join Mum sat on the beach. Elizabeth opened up her special waterproof camera casing and showed us her photos.

She had some really good ones of the fish and some of us swimming. Dad had taken a photo of the two of us with fish all around us.

We dried ourselves, put sun lotion and our hats on, and moved back into the shade.

The palm leaves swayed and the sun dappled through them to slowly tan us as we relaxed and looked out at the sea.

Hours passed and it was soon lunch time, so we put our books and iPads in our bags and made our way to the restaurant. We kept it light and drank lots of water.

We returned to Nifty and went out onto the deck again to relax in the shade, to read, or go into the sea; whatever we wanted to do. Time was ours!

The following days were almost a repeat of the first but without Mrs Archer coming near us! I guess Dad was right—she was possibly going around the island looking at each photo trying to compare each shot.

I did wonder how she was going to react when we returned to home and our Nifty home had vanished from the walkway!

Elizabeth and I took lots of photos of the gardens and the flowers and general views of the island as we walked around it.

The holiday had passed so quickly, as it can when every day was as wonderful as these had been.

We told the reception that we would be moving on after lunch.

They asked if we would require any help with our luggage.

"No, thanks. We have our own arrangements," said Dad.

Yep. We've got Nifty!

We tidied up our things, placed everything into cases and bags, and then sat down in the lounge.

"We're ready, Nifty. And what a wonderful place. Thank you for sharing this with us."

Nifty shook and the sea view dissolved into the colour of our garage, and we were home.

We unloaded our things and took them inside.

Mum was last to leave and I heard her talking to Nifty.

"Thank you, Nifty. We have some wonderful memories, and they're all down to you."

She came towards us as we stood by the garage door.

"I'm so happy that we can do these sort of trips, and more so now that I know Nifty is part of my family. With Nifty able to take us anywhere, I'm over the moon with all of the possibilities."

Nifty started to shake.

"No, Nifty!" Mum shouted. "I don't want to go to the moon. It was just an expression."

Nifty stopped shaking, and his lights flashed on and off, like he was laughing at his own joke.

Mum and the rest of us laughed as we turned the lights off in the garage and went into the house.

"Good night, Nifty," I said. "Rest well until our next adventure."

Then the thought came to me...Could we go to the moon?

THE END

UNTIL THE NEXT EXTRAORDINARY ADVENTURE...

Editing & Production
Global Wordsmiths
& Global Words Press

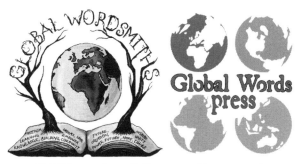

What's Your Story?

www.globalwords.co.uk
info@globalwords.co.uk